Becoming Kirsty-Lee

Also by Zenda Vecchio and published by Ginninderra Press

Mavis
A Conversation with Emily
Children at the Gate
Tiger! Tiger!
Light on Dark Water
The Swan's Egg
Spindrift
Spotted Leaves

Zenda Vecchio

Becoming Kirsty-Lee

To my friend Kate, who always believed in me

Becoming Kirsty-Lee
ISBN 978 1 74027 735 8
Copyright © text Zenda Vecchio 2012
Cover artwork: Sonja Barfoed
Cover colourwork: Wesley Hobday

First published 2012
Reprinted 2016

GINNINDERRA PRESS
PO Box 3461 Port Adelaide 5015
www.ginninderrapress.com.au

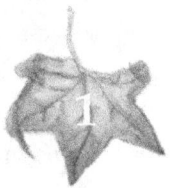

I don't know how to begin. It doesn't make sense. Everything used to be one way and now it's another and I don't see how anyone can expect us to go on as if nothing has happened.

Ordinary. We were ordinary. Like everyone else. Mum and Dad and Rose and me and Toby. I never minded. I liked it. I thought we all did. Dad never said. This morning when he left for work, he must have known but he never said anything. He kissed Mum, grinned at us, 'See you later, girls, gotta rush', paused by Toby's highchair to tousle his hair and then he was out the door. He was whistling. It was just like always.

But now…now…Mum says he's left us. She waits till Rose gets home from school too; then she tells us both. 'He's found someone else,' she says, her lips quivering. All at once her face seems to fall in on itself and she and Rose are sobbing in each other's arms.

'What do you mean, left us? How can he?' I ask. I don't cry, though; I'm too angry. 'And what about Toby? What about Toby, Mum? What are we going to tell him when Dad doesn't come home?'

At the sound of his name, my little brother looks up from his Matchbox cars and his wide, dark eyes search each of our faces in turn. He doesn't understand what's happening so he runs to Mum, whimpering, and clutches at her skirt.

Suddenly I can't bear it. I go outside to the garden. I watch a pair of wattle birds among the grevilleas. They turn themselves upside down trying to get the nectar out of the flowers. Then, suddenly startled, one flies up with a harsh cry and I turn away, shuddering. Until Toby was born, I'd been my father's favourite. He used to take me to the garage where he worked. 'Kit's as good as a boy,' he'd say proudly, his arm around my shoulders. He'd get me to help him. I'd sweep the floor, tidy up, hand him his tools. Things like that. It made me feel important.

But then Toby was born and he had a son. He didn't need me any more. He didn't actually say it, not in words, but I'd see it in his face when he bent over Toby's cot. He stopped taking me with him. It's like I wasn't there any more. I sigh. As far as I'm concerned, he left me then. When I was eleven. Two years ago.

This is different. I know that. This is worse because it's all of us. The feeling's the same, though. I'm sorry for Mum and Rose and Toby. But they'll get used to it. After all, I've had to.

***

Dad's things have gone. He must have come for them while we were at school. The house feels empty. I run from room to room. The furniture's still there of course but there's little things missing. Books. The barometer Rose and I gave him for Christmas last year. His soccer trophies. Photographs. His shaving things from the bathroom. His old work boots. He kept them by the back door, ready for gardening on the weekend…

I go slowly back to the kitchen where Rose's helping Mum with the tuna casserole for tea. Mum looks up but she doesn't say anything. Her face has got all tight and pinched as if she's expecting me to ask something and hopes I won't. Rose does, though.

She stops stirring the cheese sauce and takes a step or two towards Mum. 'Oh, Mum,' she whispers. 'Oh, Mum, what are we going to do?' She doesn't wait for Mum to answer, though. She puts her hand up to her mouth and runs out of the room. She's crying again.

I go over to the fridge and pour myself a glass of milk. I lift it to my lips but all at once I can't drink it. I watch myself put the glass carefully back on the counter. Then I pick up my backpack and go into the room I share with Rose and shut the door. For the first time I'm glad I've got homework to do.

***

I don't tell anyone at school what's happening. It's got nothing to do with them. I eat my lunch on the classroom steps and then I play soccer with the boys. They don't mind. I'm one of their best players. Boys are better than girls anyway. They don't ask questions.

I think Amy Murphy knows, though. Her sister Sophie is in Year Twelve with Rose. She tries to say something at recess but I pretend I don't know what she's on about. Her face changes then. Her lips go thin and she tosses her head and I smile to myself. She's showing her true self. I've never liked Amy Murphy, or her sister Sophie either, for that matter. Just because Rose is friends with Sophie and is always inviting her over doesn't mean I have to hang round with Amy. You'd think by now she would have worked that out. It isn't something I particularly want to tell her but if she keeps bothering me I will.

***

Mum cuts Toby's toast into careful fingers. 'You'll have to help me this weekend, girls,' she says. 'The land agent's coming on Monday to appraise the house.'

Rose puts down her mug. It clatters against the table and I stare at it, surprised.

'Land agent? Mum, what...'

'Don't start, Rose,' Mum says wearily. 'Your father's gone to a lawyer. He can't get a divorce yet, he has to wait a year for that, but he can have a property settlement. So that's what he's insisting on. A property settlement. Immediately.'

'But...' Rose begins, 'that's not... Mum, what does it mean, a property settlement. It sounds...' She knows, though. It's in her face.

I take another slice of toast and spread it thickly with honey so I don't have to look at either of them.

'It's...well, we work out which of us is going to have...you know, furniture and, and the car. They're assets and we each...'

'But the house. You can't do that with the house. It's ours. We live here and...'

I watch Rose's agitated hands. It's like I'm not there, not part of it, just a spectator. Rose's hands are like her. Elegant. Mine are square and brown and…

I hear my own voice say, 'Have we got a lawyer too?' and I'm surprised how calm I sound. Matter of fact, when all the time…

Mum shakes her head. 'No. I…'

'You'll have to get one,' I say briskly. 'If he's got one, we'll have to have one too.'

'Kit…'

'She's right, Mum,' Rose says, nodding. 'Otherwise, well it isn't fair and…'

'Fair,' Mum repeats. 'Fair.' She looks from one to the other of us. Her lips start to quiver but she tightens them resolutely. 'I never thought it'd come to this,' she whispers. 'I never thought he'd…'

'Well, he has,' I say harshly. 'And it's got nothing to do with fair. He's left us. Rose is right. I don't see why he should get the house.'

Rose picks up her mug again but she doesn't drink from it. She just holds it in both hands. 'Mum?' she says again. 'You can't let him have the house. It, it doesn't matter about the other things but the house… We live here. We've always lived here and…'

Mum gets up. She takes her plate to the sink and stands with her back to us. 'We have to sell the house,' she says. 'It belongs to both of us. That's what the lawyer said. Joint ownership. Your father… He needs his share of the money. He and…and Isla, they want a place of their own.'

I jump up too then. 'What about us?' I shout. 'What about what we want? Isn't anyone going to ask us what we want?'

I push back my chair and, head down, run to the door. I wrench it open and I'm outside. It's safe there. The grass. The trees. Mum's flowers. I fling myself down under the ash tree and clench my hands to keep from crying. I won't let myself cry. Rose cries. She cries all the time now. So does my mother. But I'm not going to. I'm not.

**

8

I wake up suddenly. I've remembered Miranda Fairweather. Her parents got divorced last year. It was very sudden. She and her little sister went to Queensland with their mother but Robbie Fairweather didn't. His father kept him. I still see him sometimes when I'm riding my bike after school.

What if Dad decides he wants Toby? Toby's his son. He waited a long time for him. What if Dad suddenly decides…?

I sit up. 'Rose,' I whisper urgently. 'Rose.'

But Rose is asleep. Mum. Mum'll know. I get out of bed and go to her room. The light's on. Once I see it, I feel better. All the darkness and Mum's brave bedside lamp. I take a deep breath but Mum's not asleep. She's just lying there. She turns her head when she hears me. I can't see her face properly, the light's not strong enough, just a tangle of shadows that's her hair and her eyes.

'Kit.'

'I…' I run to her. 'Oh, Mum, Mum what if Dad takes Toby? What if he thinks that's fair too? You have Rose an' me cos we're girls so he ought to have Toby?'

Mum reaches for me and it's like I'm little again. 'Sssh, Kit, ssh. That's not going to happen. We've already talked about that. Or the lawyers have. He…he's leaving you all with me.'

I don't feel better, though. I feel worse. Dad ought to want Toby. Even if he doesn't want Rose and me, he ought to want his own son.

My chest hurts so I can't breathe properly. 'Mum,' I whisper. 'Mum.'

She moves over and I climb into bed next to her. She puts her arms around me. It feels good, her holding me. Safe. I move closer. I pretend I'm little again like Toby and let myself fall asleep in her arms.

***

Mum's lawyer is called Mr Rhys-Matthews. When Mum goes to see him, I look after Toby. We play on the floor with his Matchbox cars. I build roads with his blocks and Toby pushes his cars along them, singing to himself. Sometimes, if Mum's late and he gets tired, I snuggle him onto my lap and I sit there, holding him. It feels good. I lean my cheek against his hair and close my eyes. I don't let myself think. I just let myself feel.

I whisper things to Toby. Secrets. 'You don't have to worry,' I say. 'I'm here. I'm going to look after you.'

The room is full of shadows. I shiver then. It's as if my father's there too, listening.

I lift my chin and tighten my arms around my brother. I say the words out loud so my father can hear. 'You can depend on me, Toby. Whatever happens, you'll always have me.'

**

I wake up a lot at night now, though I never used to. I never used to mind the dark either. I curl myself up very small and shut my eyes but it doesn't help. I can still feel the dark out there, waiting. It's full of things I don't want to think about.

My father. Isla. Mum told us that's why he left. Because of Isla. He wants to be with her instead of us. I clench my hands so hard that my nails bite into my palms. I do it on purpose. Sometimes if the pain's bad enough it blocks everything else out. It doesn't always work though. I have to keep doing more and more bad things to myself to stop myself from thinking.

My father used to be so proud of us. He kept a photo of us in his wallet. When I helped him at the garage, he was always showing it off to the other men.

It doesn't make sense. I don't understand how Isla can suddenly be more important than all of us. Mum and Rose and Toby and me. I don't understand any of it.

I hate him. I hate both of them but I hate him most. I open my eyes and say it out loud. For a moment, hearing myself, I feel strong and powerful but then my voice starts to waver and in the end I'm crying. Because that's what the dark does. It gets inside you and confuses you and in the end it makes you helpless. The pain in my hands isn't powerful enough to make it stop.

The daytime's all right. It's easy then. When I'm with Mum and Rose and Toby, I can be proud and defiant and pretend I don't care. But at night I'm all by myself and I remember things.

I don't want to. I don't want to have to think about him at all.

***

Sam MacIntyre is my best friend. He has been ever since we started school together. I want to tell him about my father but I don't know how to start. Things have got sort of complicated with us lately. I know why. It's the new girl, Michaela Thornton. All the boys like her. She's got these long, tanned legs and big, dewy eyes and a funny, whispery voice. I don't mind Sam liking her. Not really. But he likes her for all the wrong reasons, not because she's clever or funny or good at soccer, not proper reasons like that. He likes her because she's a girl, the right kind of girl. He hasn't got time for me any more. I'm not pretty. I've got red hair and freckles and everyone keeps telling me I frown too much.

We used to go down to the oval after school and play soccer but now he goes off with Jason instead. They hang around Michaela's house hoping she'll come out and talk to them. It's pathetic. And they're not the only ones. Yesterday I saw Ryan go with them too. I would have thought Sam had more sense. I bet Michaela doesn't like any of them. She's too far up herself to bother with them

That's what I mean. Everything's changed. It's not just my father. Everything else has changed too.

Someone wants to buy the house. The land agent comes round to tell us after tea. She's smiling all over her face. 'A very reasonable offer, Mrs Forrester,' she says to Mum. 'I'm sure you agree with me. Not quite as much as you hoped, perhaps, but Mr and Mrs Morrison are cash buyers, which is always an advantage, especially in a situation like yours.'

'Yes,' says Mum. She doesn't look at the land agent, though. She looks at her hands in her lap. 'I thought it would take longer. Just two weeks. I thought it would take months. I…I haven't got used to things yet.'

The land agent's lips stretch into another smile. It doesn't mean anything to her. 'I take it you will be accepting this offer then?'

Mum nods. 'I guess so. I'll have to consult with my…' Her hands twist in her lap but then she lifts her head. 'Yes,' she says steadily. 'Yes, of course. Tell the Morrisons we accept.'

After the land agent leaves, Rose and Mum look at one another helplessly.

'Now what happens?' I ask. I'm picking up Toby's toys. I've got into the habit of tidying up after him all the time. I've found out you can get used to anything. Even living in a house that looks like one of those you see in magazines.

Mum hesitates. 'I…I don't know. It's a bad time to sell. Once your father's got his share…'

'Oh, Mum.' Rose's voice wavers. 'Oh, Mum.'

I look at them both. 'Dad shouldn't get any,' I say. 'He left us. Anyway, Isla ought to get them a house and if I was Mr Rhys-Matthews, that's what I'd have told him.'

'Oh, Kit, don't be silly. Isla…well, who knows what will happen with your father and Isla? You don't understand, Kit. He might… He still might…' She drops her head and fidgets with her fingers in her lap again.

I know what she's thinking. I know what they're both thinking. They hope Dad'll change his mind. They hope he'll get sick of Isla and come back. He won't. I know he won't. And even if he did, it's too late now. The house is sold. The Morrisons are going to live here.

I remember them. They came last week with the land agent when Mum was out and I had to let them in. They had a baby and a fat little girl with glasses and Mr Morrison kept writing notes on a clipboard. I take a deep breath. I don't want to think about it. They're going to live in our house. The little girl will probably have our room, mine and Rose's, she'll play in our garden and…Rose and my mother are stupid. It's because of my father this is all happening and they keep wanting him to come back. I don't. I never want to see him again.

Very carefully, I put Toby's truck in his toy box and close the lid. Then I turn and go outside. I get my bike out of the shed and climb on. The wind's cool on my hot face. I concentrate on pedaling. Up and down. Up and down. I stand up so I can pump harder. It feels good. Like flying. I close my eyes just for a moment and, even though I know it's dangerous, I don't care.

When it's almost dark, I turn my bike around and ride slowly home. Behind me, where the sun's setting, the sky looks bruised and I carry a picture of it in my mind as I put my bike away. For some reason it makes me feel better.

***

My grandparents have a dairy farm in the hills near Woodleigh. It's called Rockvale. Next week we're going there to live.

Rose is relieved. 'I thought we'd have to go somewhere else,' she tells me when we're getting ready for bed. 'You know, somewhere where we didn't know anyone, where we'd have to begin all over again. But Rockvale…I've always liked it there. And we'll have Belinda and Emma. It'll be like having two more sisters.'

I start to unplait my hair. 'It'll be awfully crowded. Gran and Grandpa, Uncle Fred and Auntie Evie as well as the cousins.'

'And Ash,' Rose adds. 'I don't expect he counts, though.'

I'd forgotten about Ash. Most people do. He's some sort of relative of Auntie Evie, a nephew I think. He came to Rockvale a few years ago after a car accident. Gran says it's damaged him. You can see that because his face is all scarred and he limps when he walks. But I think Gran means something else. I think she's talking about the way he is inside. She makes too much of it, though. It isn't important. Ash just doesn't like people very much and I don't blame him. I'm beginning to feel the same way.

Rose slips her nightie over her head and pauses to check her reflection in the mirror. 'What do you think school will be like in the country?' she asks. 'It's a long way away, of course, so we'll have to go by bus. Remember at Christmas, Belinda telling us about the bus and how Matt Heiland kept saving her a seat even though she didn't want to sit with him.'

I sigh. I wish Rose would be quiet. She's making me nervous. Anyway, I don't like thinking about Christmas. It was only a few weeks after Christmas, when school had just started again, that we came home and Mum said... It doesn't feel right. It's only the beginning of March but already it feels like years ago.

I'm not sure I'm going to like it at Rockvale. There'll be such a lot to get used to. All the relatives. A new school. There probably won't be anywhere I can ride my bike either, no shops or oval, just trees and grass and...and cows. I've never liked cows much. Horses, it'd be different if it were horses...

I get into bed and pick up my library book. Rose clicks her tongue against her teeth in exasperation but she knows better than to try and get me to talk when I don't want to.

***

We're leaving for Rockvale tomorrow. Everything is packed. Most of our furniture has been sold because there won't be room for it there.

'But...but aren't we ever going to have a place of our own again?' I say. 'I mean Rockvale's all right for a while but...'

Mum bites her lip. 'Oh, Kit,' she says. Then she looks away and I don't ask any more because I know the answer.

I go outside and sit on the back step. Even the garden's different. The lawn is overgrown and untidy and the cotoneaster needs pruning. There's no water in the birdbath, just green scum. All the summer flowers have died because no one has watered them. Suddenly, I jump up. I have to find Sam. I can't go without telling him. All those years when we were best friends, they have to mean something even if...even if...

Sam's mooching around on his bike. As soon as I catch sight of him, I start to run after him. 'Hey, Sam. Wait up a minute, Sam,' and he skids to a stop. I'm quite casual. 'I've been meaning to tell you,' I say. 'We're leaving tomorrow. We're going to live near Woodleigh.' I'm proud of myself. I say it just like I might say I was going to the oval or the library.

Sam's shocked. 'Woodleigh? What on earth are you going there for? It's so far away. Amy Murphy said you were getting a place near here and I thought...'

'My grandparents live near there. You know that. Remember when we took you to Rockvale for the day. And now Dad's gone, well, we have to live somewhere. We can't afford to stay here.' I toss my head. 'Mum says it's for the best.'

Sam looks miserable. He scruffs at the dirt with the toe of his sneaker. 'But, Kit, I...'

I don't let him finish. 'Don't call me Kit,' I say. 'I'm Kirsty-Lee now.'

He knows that's my proper name of course. Everyone does. But no one's ever used it, not even my teachers. I've been Kit ever since my father started calling me that when I was a baby. But not any more. I don't want to be called Kit any more.

Sam's face goes red. 'I'm sorry you're going.' He gulps and starts fiddling with his hand brakes. 'Oh, Kit, I'll miss you.'

I don't say anything. I can't. But I'm glad we're no longer proper friends otherwise leaving him would hurt too much. As it is...well, it doesn't really matter very much. He'll forget about me quickly enough, especially now he's got Michaela to think about.

15

We've been here nearly three weeks. It's different from when we stayed for holidays because we were guests then. Now we have to join in and be part of the family. At least that's what Grandpa said the first night. 'You belong here now, Beth,' he said. 'You and your children.' Rose ran to him and kissed him but I didn't. I wasn't sure. I'm still not.

It's different for Mum and Rose and Toby. They fit in. Mum's happier. I can see that. Some of the prettiness has even come back into her face. She's still sad but it's like the sadness has got quieter. And Rose has changed too. She's always changing and it confuses me. I get used to her one way and then she goes and changes and I have to begin all over again.

She's so excited about sharing things with Emma and Belinda. 'We're all sisters now,' she says and makes me sit with them on the bus. It's stupid, though. It's a kind of pretending. All they do is giggle and whisper to one another and fuss about what they look like. I think I liked Rose better before, even if she kept running off crying.

'You ought to let me do your hair for you, Kirsty-Lee,' says Belinda. 'You're too old for plaits.'

I frown. 'I like…' I begin but I don't get to finish.

'Oh, give up, Belinda. Give up now,' says Rose, interrupting. 'Kirsty-Lee won't let you do her hair. I've been on at her for ages but it's a waste of time. She doesn't care how she looks.'

Belinda takes no notice. She turns to me again. 'You've got really pretty hair, Kirsty-Lee. I noticed it last night when you were brushing it. You ought to get it cut and wear it loose. That's what I'd do if it were mine. It's a pity to hide it in those tight, horrible plaits.'

I look carefully at Belinda but her face seems innocent enough. I feel my mouth get tight. She hasn't realised yet. She hasn't realised I'm the wrong kind of girl. No matter what I do to try and change my appearance, I'll always be the wrong kind of girl. I know that. As soon as I saw Sam MacIntyre's face when he looked at Michaela Thornton, I knew what it meant.

I lift my head. 'At least I look like myself,' I say with dignity. 'You three look like clones.' My lip curls. 'Barbie doll clones.'

It's true. They do look like that. The same long, fair hair, the same blue eyes and pink cheeks. Emma flushes and I feel suddenly ashamed. Emma's quieter than Rose and Belinda but, apart from that, she's just the same. She's got this thing about Petey Wilson. As soon as he gets on the bus, she goes all red and drops her books and tries not to look at him. It's pathetic.

I get up and stalk to the front of the bus. It's better there. Quieter. I lift my chin and look fierce so no one will dare sit next to me.

Rose tells Mum, though. She comes in when I'm finishing my homework. 'Kit,' she begins. Then she remembers. 'Kirsty-Lee, what is it? The girls say you won't sit with them on the bus any more. They say you won't sit with anyone even though some of the other kids have tried to be friendly.'

I feel the blood rush into my cheeks but I manage to keep my voice steady. 'You don't have to worry, Mum. I'm fine.'

'No. No, you're not, Kirsty-Lee. I know you're not and I think...'

I duck my head. 'I like sitting by myself,' I whisper. My chest is so tight, I can hardly breathe. I keep my eyes on my clenched hands and will her to go away.

At last I hear her get up and start towards the door but, before she gets there, she pauses. 'Kirsty-Lee, if something's bothering you, I wish you'd tell me. I know it's hard for you, adjusting, but I'm your mother and I understand, really I do and...' She waits for me to say something but when I don't, she gives up, closing the door quietly behind her

I go over to the window and stand there, staring out. I can see the sky. Above the low, distant hills, the first stars are coming out, little pinpricks of light. Watching them, I become calm again.

Then I start to remember. Not about Dad. I never let myself think about him. But afterwards. I remember sitting on the floor with Toby on my lap waiting for Mum to come home. I remember the feel of his hair, silky-soft against my cheek, and the last of the light like ribbons across the faded carpet. I knew who I was then. Toby's sister. And…and Mum. Mum needed me. She kept telling me. 'I'm glad I've got you, Kit,' she'd say, sinking down into the nearest chair while I hurried to make her a cup of tea. 'I don't know what I'd do without you.' Rose too. When we were getting ready for bed, Rose talked to me, she really talked as if…as if what I thought, as if what I thought mattered.

I bite at the inside of my cheek. It's not like that any more. Mum's got Gran and Auntie Evie and Rose has got the cousins. Even Toby. I feel my eyes start to sting and clench my hands quickly. Toby's changed most of all. It's like suddenly he's stopped being a baby and become a little boy. He follows Uncle Fred and Grandpa around all day. They take him out in the ute to check on the cows and if he gets tired they make a place for him to sleep on a hessian bag among the hay bales. Sometimes I think he's forgotten who I am just like he's forgotten Dad. He never asks for him any more…

I take a deep breath and stare hard at the stars. Then I make them a promise. It isn't any use remembering things, not bad things or good ones either. They weaken you. I tighten my mouth. I'm going to work things out. I'm going to work things out by myself. I don't need anyone else. They mean well, I know that, but you can't depend on them because they don't understand. Not really. In the end you can only depend on yourself.

I feel suddenly strong. Invincible. It's a good word. I put my hand out and touch the windowpane. It's quite cold. 'Invincible,' I say again and I trace the word on the glass in front of me so I won't forget it.

***

I teach the new calf how to drink from a bucket. Ash tells me what to do. I let her suck my fingers. Then, very carefully, I lower my hand into the milk. The calf coughs and splutters and jerks her head up. Her eyes are frantic. I'm sorry for her. She's hungry but she doesn't know what to do. She wants her mother.

'All right, girl,' I say. 'It's all right. You can trust me.'

We begin again. After a while the calf gets the idea and drinks most of the milk. I laugh and look at Ash in triumph.

'Good,' he says. 'Good.' He doesn't smile or anything but he helps me put the calf back in the pen with the others. 'Tonight,' he says. 'Tonight, after school, you'll have to feed her again. She's your responsibility now.'

I nod and give an excited little skip. Then I run to get ready to catch the bus with the others.

***

I like writing in here. I'm surprised because I've never liked writing things for school. But this is different. It's private. I like putting the things I think down on paper. I live in two different worlds now. The outside one is full of confusion and I have no control over it. But here, inside myself, it is quiet. Ordered. The way I want.

At night, when Emma and Rose and Belinda are whispering secrets in the dark, I turn over in my bed to face the wall and plan out things to write. It stops me from feeling lonely.

They've made me a room. I can hardly believe it. Uncle Fred and Ash and Grandpa have been working for days to enclose part of the back veranda. They've lined the walls with wood panels and resurfaced the floor and made a little oblong window. The window's all overgrown with ivy. Uncle Fred says he'll soon have it pulled out but I don't want him to.

'I like it like that,' I tell him. 'See how it makes the light all green and wavery. It's like we're underwater.'

Auntie Evie has put up curtains, white with bright yellow stripes, but I'm never going to pull them across. They've made me some furniture too, a cupboard and a shelf and Ash has found me an old table I can use for a desk.

'It's not much, I know, Kirsty-Lee,' says Mum apologetically. 'Everything's a bit makeshift but I thought you might like a place of your own.'

I put my arms around her and kiss her. 'I love it,' I whisper. 'It's…it's beautiful.'

It is too. The walls are all white and they've painted the furniture yellow and Gran's got me this funny, furry rug thing to put by my bed because the floor's just cement and she's worried I'll be cold. Everyone gives me things and I put them carefully on my shelf. A spider plant from Emma. A scented candle from Belinda. A brass horse that she found in a second-hand shop from Rose.

Even Toby's done me a special picture. ''S a cow,' he says, holding it out.

I nod solemnly and blu-tack it above my desk.

I look around at everyone. There's a sort of shining in their faces and my throat chokes up. I want to thank them but I can't. The words won't come.

Gran says it for me, though. 'It's all right, Kirsty-Lee,' she says. 'We just want you to feel at home with us. And Grandpa and I were getting worried, you sharing with the girls. With all that talking, we were sure you weren't getting enough sleep.'

Everyone laughs. I run to Gran and hug her. She feels so soft. She smells nice too, of cinnamon and vanilla and baby powder. I hope she knows how grateful I am. I hope they all do.

Then they leave. I'm alone. I look around me at my perfect, perfect room.

I start to cry. I don't know why. They're funny tears though. There's no pain in them. They slide down my cheeks and I feel…I feel all hushed and trembly like it's early morning and the first birds have just begun to sing…

***

As soon as I get home from school, I help Ash with the calves. Then I pack up the cake and biscuits Gran's left out for me and call the old dog Mandy. We go exploring till we find a good place for our picnic. Mandy's so old her muzzle has gone white and her eyes are starting to film over but she likes sitting in the sun with me. We watch the wind in the grass, the sky, a flock of grey and pink galahs. Once we even see a snake, a dark shudder, and then it's gone. Mandy pricks up her ears but she doesn't move or bark or anything. She's too old now to care. I put my face against her fur and whisper to her. She's been a good dog. She's worked hard all her life. And now she's waiting. My hand, fondling her ears, stops and she turns her head to look at me, surprised. I know what she's waiting for. I know and I don't want to think about it.

I get up suddenly and start to run. I run as fast as I can. Mandy doesn't come with me. She stays sitting in the sun. She knows she can't keep up with me.

In one of the trees by the abandoned pump house there's an old swing. I stare at it for a moment. I ought to go back and get Toby. He'd like it. But I don't. Quite suddenly, I want it for myself. I test the ropes. They feel strong enough so I get on. I start to bend my legs backwards and forwards. Years ago my father took me to the playground whenever Rose and Mum went shopping. He showed me how to work my legs so I could make the swing go by myself. I haven't forgotten. I go higher and higher. It's like flying. It's better than riding my bike with my eyes shut. I laugh. I'm like a little kid. I'm a bird, a swallow. There are swallows in the hay shed. Ash showed me the place above the door where they make a nest each spring. Welcome swallows, he said. I'd like to be a welcome swallow. They know where they belong. They know their way home. I tilt my head back and stare into the blue, descending sky.

I see Mandy creep out of the shadow of the trees, her head hanging down. She's come to look for me. She's my dog now. That's what Ash says. She's chosen you, he said, you're her friend. He says it like it's an honour, like her choosing me makes me special. I stop swinging and call to her.

'It's getting late, Mandy,' I tell her. 'We have to go back.'

She follows me to the house. Uncle Fred and Grandpa are coming in from the milking. I catch up with them. I still feel like a little kid, like Toby. Content. Night's coming. Everything's all right. Mandy goes to her place under the back veranda. She's always slept there. I'm glad because it's close to my room and when I wake up at night and can't sleep, I know she's there, guarding me.

***

Every morning, before school, after I've helped Ash with the calves, we load the ute with hay and take it out to the cows in the paddock. I like doing things with Ash. He never says more than he has to and neither do I. It's good to be with someone who appreciates silence.

The ute bumps over the track, the sky's all hushed and solemn, the cows lift their heads and stare at us. I feel something inside me expanding, reaching out. I turn to Ash. His expression doesn't change but he knows how I feel. I know he does.

***

I tell Ash about the swing. I tell him how it's like flying and he nods but he doesn't say anything.

Ash's face is all scarred from the car accident. When I first came, he'd flinch away if I looked at him. It was as if just looking hurt his skin. But it's all right now. He's used to me.

Kids at school, I've heard them say things about Ash. At first I thought I ought to say something back. Get angry. But Ash is Ash. He wouldn't want me to. That's why silence is so important. It's a shield. Something to hold on to.

I wait for Ash to give me the milk for Bambi. That's what I've called my calf. Ash smiles when I tell him. I know why. Cows aren't elegant like deer. But I don't mind Ash smiling though I would if it were anyone else. It's sort of good. I've never seen Ash smile before not even at Toby. When I smile back, it's special. It's like in soccer once when I kicked the winning goal from a penalty shot. A dizziness.

Ash puts his fingers through the fence and lets Bambi suck them while I go in the gate with the bucket.

School's all right. It isn't any different from before. I guess all schools are pretty much the same. As soon as I'm old enough, I'm leaving anyway. They've already taught me all I need to know. I can read. Once you can read, you can find out everything else you need to know from the library. If it isn't in a book, they've got it on the computer. The best thing is maths. I've suddenly got good at it. It's a surprise because I didn't used to be at primary school. But high school maths is exciting, it's algebra and geometry as well and they're sort of fascinating. I didn't know you could do so much with numbers. They don't change either. Once you've learned the rules they stay the same. Not like English and poetry where everyone has a different opinion about what it means.

I'm not sure how useful it's all going to be, though. Even simple things like the area of a circle πr^2. I can't think of any situation where I'm ever going to need to know that. I asked Rose and she just shrugged and shook her head. Rose stopped doing maths last year. She said it was too hard. She does things like home economics and history and graphic design, which is a boring kind of art where you don't draw pictures but make labels for bottles of wine and things instead. I don't know why she bothers. If I could draw like Rose, I'd draw horses and birds and a newborn calf struggling to its feet. There'd be some point in that.

Rose has got really enthusiastic about joining things. She tried out for the lacrosse team but she wasn't good enough so she has to compromise with debating. It's Belinda's idea. 'Ben Wilson's good at debating,' she says, looking sly. Rose blushes. She likes Ben Wilson, though she pretends she doesn't.

Belinda looks round at the rest of us, frowning. 'If Rose and I do debating,' she says, 'we'll have to stay late on Tuesdays. Do you think someone could get us afterwards in the car? It wouldn't take that long.'

'Of course,' says Auntie Evie, getting up and starting to clear away the tea dishes. 'If I can't, then I'm sure Beth will.'

My mother nods. She's pleased. She always wanted Rose to join in things at school but Rose never would. 'It'd be all right if Kit could come too,' she'd say, twisting her hands together. 'But she's too young. You know she is, Mum.'

It's different now. She's got Belinda. I catch them smiling at one another and get up quickly to help Auntie Evie with the dishes.

On Tuesdays Emma and I have to catch the bus home by ourselves. I go down the back to sit with her. It'd be mean to ignore her and sit by myself. Emma's all right. She reminds me of Toby sometimes, though I don't quite know why. Maybe it's the way she smiles, sort of slow, like she has to think about it first. She's always hiding behind her hair too. It's darker than Rose and Belinda's. Caramel coloured, I think, screwing up my eyes and frowning, a bit like a fawn, one of those spotted ones you see in television documentaries. I smile at the idea, pleased, and decide to write it down in my book as soon as I get home. Because that is what's she's like. A fawn. Shy and delicate and easily hurt. Belinda's not. She's sharp and bright like one of those glittery stones you find sometimes in the scrub.

I've never really thought much about people before. Not about what they're like inside. It's hard. It's even harder when you love someone. Like Rose. I don't really know what Rose is like. She seems all soft and gentle but... You'd think, if you loved someone, it would be easy. But it isn't. The love gets in the way and sort of hides them from you.

Like Dad. We all thought we knew him. But we didn't. He wasn't who we thought he was.

***

Emma knocks at my door. She wants to know if she can do her homework with me. 'Belinda and Rose talk too much,' she says. 'I can't concentrate.' She ducks her head then. She's embarrassed because she thinks she's said something bad about them.

I watch her fiddle with the broken strap of her backpack while she waits for me to answer. I suck on my pen. I'm not sure I want her in my room. Still…

'All right,' I say, shrugging.

Emma settles herself in my easy chair with her books. She doesn't say anything, just opens her history book and starts to read. I get back to my maths. When I've finished, I glance across at her. She's got her legs curled under her and she's leaning forward so her hair falls to one side like a curtain. It shines gold in the light from my lamp.

All at once she lifts her head and catches my eye. She smiles. It feels good, her being in my room. Friendly. She gets up then and goes to the shelf where the spider plant she gave me's growing. It's got a lot of tiny new leaves. They're striped like the others but they're darker too and they've got a gloss to them like they've been polished.

Emma reaches up and touches them one by one. 'This is a good room, Kirsty-Lee,' she says. 'You're lucky.'

I look around me. I know what she means. The room she shares with Belinda and Rose is cramped and fussy. They've got pink frilled bedspreads and pictures on the walls and Rose's collection of porcelain dolls along the window sill. There's no room to be yourself in it.

I say quickly, 'I know and I…' but then I stop. Because…because if we hadn't come to Rockvale, maybe they'd have made this room for her, maybe they'd already planned it, Ash and Grandpa and Uncle Fred, and that's why it didn't take them very long. They had everything ready and were just waiting for the cows to finish calving so they'd have time to begin.

I turn back to my desk. I pick up my pen and start doodling in the margin of my environmental studies book. 'Emma,' I say at last. 'Emma, do you mind us being here?' I force myself to look at her. 'I mean, if we'd stayed home, maybe, maybe they'd have made this room for you.'

The colour floods into her cheeks and she looks down. 'Kirsty-Lee, I…' Then she shakes her head.

'I wouldn't blame you if you did, Emma. I think…I think I'd mind if I were you. There's such a lot of us…and the house isn't really big enough and…'

'No,' Emma steps forward and lays her hand on my arm. 'No, Kirsty-Lee. It isn't like that.' Her eyes are very blue and they meet mine without flinching. 'I'm glad you all came.' She laughs a little. 'It's exciting. Sort of like a book. All of us together. Auntie Beth is so nice and Rose and little Toby, I just love him and you, oh, Kirsty-Lee, how could I mind, my own cousins…'

Belonging, I think. For Emma it is as simple as that. We are her cousins. We belong to her. But I'm not so sure.

After Emma goes to bed, I lie awake for a long time. Mum and me and Rose and Toby and Dad. We used to be a family. We used to belong together. But now Dad wants Isla. He wants to be with her instead of us. It changes things. It changes everything.

Mum and Rose, they think it's all right like this. They think we can begin again. But we can't. I know we can't.

I think if I'm not careful I might start to love Emma. But I don't want to. If you love someone, you give them parts of yourself and that's dangerous. If they go away, they take part of you with them. I don't want that to happen. I don't want to lose any more of myself.

6

It's the end of autumn and all the leaves have changed colour. The liquidambars behind the house look like they're on fire. They glow red and burgundy and copper-gold. Ash and I watch the leaves fall. They're like butterflies dancing in the sun. They're so brave. They're dying and they know it but they go on with their dance anyway. Ash bends down and picks one up. He does it gently as if he knows it can still feel and the leaf, star-shaped in his hand, trembles as if it recognises him.

I go for long walks with Ash. We don't talk. We don't have to. Ash shows me all sorts of things. The honeyeaters in the flowering gums. The old stone well overgrown with ivy. The way the wind makes the silky oak's leaves turn silver. A flock of wheeling cockatoos. The river with its reeds and willows and wild ducks. A fallen tree decorated with lichen. Sounds too. Bird cries. Insects. The water in the reeds. Wilson's bull across the valley. And once, coming home from the cow shed after dark, the sharp yipping of a dog fox.

I never used to notice things. And now… The whole world has changed. Only, only I know that's not it. It's me. Truth, I think, truth. That's what I want. To see things truly. As they really are and not what other people tell me. Maths. This and this and this and together they make up the whole.

I think about Ash a lot. He hides who he is. That's what Gran meant when she said he was damaged.

Everyone here, Gran, Grandpa, Uncle Fred, Auntie Evie, Mum, they're used to Ash. They take him for granted. They don't think about him as a person. He's here and he does what he's supposed to and he doesn't like talking, so they let him be. He doesn't even have his meals with us. I'm

not sure about that. He's so alone. No one should be that alone. Except…
except…isn't that what I want. To be left alone. Only…only…

Thinking's difficult. I'm just beginning to understand that. At school
they're always urging us to think. Think for yourself, they say that all the
time, but they don't mean it. Not really. They want us to think like them.
They don't like it if you're different.

It's confusing. That's why I like writing things down. It helps. Talking's
no good. Feelings get in the way when you talk. Yours and theirs. You get
distracted.

I want to understand about Ash. It's important. His loneliness
frightens me but it makes me sad too and I don't know why. That's what
bothers me. I don't know why.

***

When we've finished with the calves, Ash says, 'Come on, Kirsty-Lee. I've
got something to show you.'

It's Saturday so we don't have to hurry. It's my favourite time of day,
early morning. The spiders' webs on the fences are hung with dew so they
gleam gold in the sun. Above us the sky is wide and blue and endless and
there's a sort of haze across all the paddocks, there's the placid cows and the
stubble of old grass and the magpies in the scramble of gums by the river.

I take Bambi's bucket back to the kitchen and follow Ash into the hay
shed.

'Look,' he says.

On a broken bale of hay there's a nest of kittens, five of them, striped
and black and ginger and one little funny-coloured one that Ash says is
tortoiseshell.

He bends down and picks her up. 'Hold out your hands, Kirsty-Lee.'

The kitten squints up her eyes and hisses and spits. She opens her pink
mouth and shows all her sharp little teeth.

'Oh. Oh, Ash.' My throat hurts. She's so tiny and defenceless but she
doesn't know it. She thinks she can scare us. My heart contracts in pity.

'I found them in here yesterday,' Ash says. 'Their mother must have shifted them from the scrub now it's getting cold.'

I nod and put the kitten back with the others.

Ash says, 'You ought to keep her, Kirsty-Lee. You could have her in your room. She'd be company for you.'

'But...but would they let me, Gran and Grandpa? I don't think they like cats. I've heard Grandpa say...'

'I asked them. I asked them last night after you were in bed. They said it would be all right. I told them how much you needed her.'

'I...' I straighten up. I look into his face. No one else does that. I've noticed. It's because of his scars, but they don't worry me. They never have. I look into his eyes. He tries to make them slide away from mine but I'm determined and I don't let him.

'Why don't you have one too?' I ask. 'You're all by yourself. I'm sure Grandpa would let you have a cat or...or a dog like Mandy. You probably don't even have to ask. You could just get one. You haven't got anything of your own at all.'

'Oh, Kirsty-Lee.' His voice falters in his throat and he shakes his head and turns away.

I watch his hands among the kittens. It's like when he picked up the liquidambar leaf. The kittens recognise him.

'You mustn't worry about me,' Ash says softly. 'I have all I need.' He looks up at me. His eyes are darker than I've ever seen them. They're like the river water where it's made a pool in the reeds. 'I've got the wind and the sky and the trees. That's all I need.'

I pick up my kitten and hold her against my cheek. She's so soft. 'You've got more than that,' I say. 'You've got me. I'm your friend.' My voice is suddenly as shaky as his and I don't dare look at him, I'm too embarrassed.

Ash doesn't answer. He starts pulling out bales of hay to load onto the ute. It hasn't rained enough yet for the grass to grow in the paddocks and we still have to feed the cows.

'Leave her with the others till we come back,' Ash says. 'Then I'll help you find a box for her to sleep in. She'll need a litter tray as well.'

I put the kitten carefully back in the nest. 'Minka,' I say. 'I'm going to call her Minka.'

Ash nods. 'Sounds good.' He throws down another bale. 'She's lucky, that kitten. All the others'll just be barn cats. She'll be special.' He smiles. It changes his whole face. 'I reckon I'm lucky too, Kirsty-Lee, real lucky.'

We don't say any more. But all at once I feel different. Light-hearted. And it's not just because of Minka.

At night Minka sleeps on my bed. Mum doesn't know. She thinks Minka sleeps in the box Ash made for her. Minka curls up till she's a perfect circle, her little pink nose hidden in her funny little tail that's got dark rings round it like a possum's. Sometimes, in the night, she creeps up and licks my hand. It tickles. Her tongue is all raspy. I feel my mouth smile in the darkness and I put my hand out to her. I can feel the life throbbing in her. She's purring. She likes it here with me. She's forgotten about her brothers and sisters in the hay. I'm glad. I don't want her to be lonely. I want her to be happy with me.

I don't like the sound of the wind. It has voices in it, sad voices, and they frighten me. I ask Ash. 'Why does the wind sound like that at night, as if it's lonely?'

Ash looks away into the distance. He's got hazel eyes but in some lights they look gold. 'The wind's lost, Kirsty-Lee,' he says. 'It doesn't know where it's going. That's why it keeps changing directions.'

Ash makes me a wind chime and we hang it on the veranda. 'Now when the wind cries, you'll be able to hear music as well,' Ash explains. 'The music will make it better.'

He's right. Ash understands about music. In the evening, he sits on the steps outside his room that is really part of the shed they've fixed up for him and plays his guitar. Sometimes his music dances like sunlight on water but mostly it's unbearably sad. He doesn't mind when I sit next to him and listen. He smiles at me and nods and goes on playing. The music gets right inside me until I ache with it. I'm never sure, though. I'm never sure whether I ache with his pain or my own.

The wind's music is different. It doesn't belong to either of us. It's free. It haunts my dreams but I like it.

***

After we've finished our homework, Emma and I play with Minka. We crumble up paper for her to pounce on. Minka's like a ballerina. She dances and twists and pirouettes. Emma gets an old ball of wool from her mother and we give it to Minka to see what she'll do. She chases it across the floor batting at it with her paw until it starts to unwind and she gets hopelessly tangled up in it. She sits still then and blinks at us in astonishment. Laughing, we bend down to rescue her

'Silly Minka,' says Emma. 'You'd better be careful. If Mum saw you like that, she'd knit you into a jumper for Grandpa.'

I giggle. 'Minka would make a better fur coat,' I say. 'Think how warm she'd be. And so pretty. All those colours.'

'Quick, Minka,' says Emma, scooping her up and kissing her. 'Quick. You'd better eat some more so we can grow you big enough to make a fur coat for Grandpa. You're so small now, you'd only make a glove. Where's your saucer? We'd better get you some more milk.'

Minka struggles, so Emma puts her down again. She's offended. She doesn't like us laughing at her. She has too much dignity. But soon she jumps back onto my lap. She can never stay mad at us for long.

***

There are no leaves left on the liquidambars. Against the evening sky, they have a defiant majesty. I go to them one after the other touching each in turn. Ash says that while trees are dormant, they go on journeys, like we do when we dream. Then, when they return, they put out little green leaves like banners to let us know they're back. I laugh but Ash's face is very serious.

'There are all sorts of journeys, Kirsty-Lee,' he says. 'We just have to decide which one's right for us.'

I reach out and touch, very gently, the nearest liquidambar. 'I know,' I say but Ash has already started to walk away and I don't think he hears.

8

When we come home from school, Auntie Evie's in the garden pruning the last few rose bushes. She calls out to Emma and Belinda so Rose and I go into the kitchen by ourselves.

Mum's in there by the sink. There's a tightness around her mouth that I haven't seen for a long time. She wipes her hands on a tea towel and says quietly, 'There's a letter for you girls, a letter from your father.'

Rose makes a sudden exclamation and runs forward, her cheeks bright pink. The letter is on the kitchen bench. I can see it there but I make no move toward it.

Rose hesitates as she picks it up. 'It's addressed to both of us, Kirsty-Lee. Do you want to come with me so we can read it together?'

I swallow. 'No,' I say. 'No, I don't care what it says.' I want my voice to sound loud and defiant but it doesn't. Instead it's just a whisper.

'Kirsty-Lee,' Mum says, looking distressed, 'Kirsty-Lee, I really think you should consider…' but I don't wait to hear the rest.

I run out of the kitchen, slamming the door behind me. I run around the house and stumble up the veranda steps to my room. It's quiet there. I lean against the door, panting. Minka's on my bed asleep. My spider plant hangs down from my shelf, its funny little tufts of leaves making spiky shadows on the wall behind. My books are all there and my collection of stones and the blue wren's feather that Ash gave me last week. It's a safe place.

I sit down in front of my desk. There's the picture above it, the funny scribble Toby insists is a cow. I remember when I first saw my room, all complete, a surprise because although I knew they were doing something to the back veranda, I didn't know they were making me a room. They were all there, Gran and Grandpa, Uncle Fred and Auntie Evie, Mum, Ash, the girls and Toby. They stood around me, smiling. My father wasn't there. He left us at the end of January. He chose to go. And now…and now…what does he want with me now? A letter. He's sent a letter. A letter to both of us, Rose and what was the other one called, oh yes, Kirsty-Lee. Only my father never called me that. He called me Kit. It was Kit who loved him, Kit who used to swing on the front gate watching for him to come home from work, Kit who went to the garage on Saturday mornings to help him with his tools, Kit who… I shut my eyes and bite down hard on my lip. I don't want to remember Kit. Even after Toby was born, she tried so hard to be the boy her father wanted but it wasn't enough, nothing she did was ever enough.

I'm Kirsty-Lee now. It took a while but I've made them all call me Kirsty-Lee, even Toby. And Kirsty-Lee is a girl and she… But I'm not sure yet who Kirsty-Lee is. Sometimes, seeing her face in the mirror, her wide dark eyes, the sprinkling of freckles across her nose, her determined mouth and tilted chin, sometimes I'm not sure that's me either. I look the same. I look like Kit but I know I'm not her any more. Only I liked being Kit. She lived at 14 Harcourt Crescent, Netherby. She was Sam MacIntrye's best friend and after school she played soccer with the boys even in summer. She had just started Year Eight and her home room teacher was called Ms Phillips and everyone said she looked just like her father…

Behind me I hear my door open and I whirl around, startled, but it's only Rose. I don't know quite who I expected. My father perhaps. In the space between one heartbeat and the next, I feel suddenly disconnected, as if I'm back there, as if I'm Kit again and none of this has happened. My father left for work only this morning, he tousled Toby's hair and went out the door whistling and now he's come home again, his arms full of surprises for us because it's Friday and he often does that, brings us little gifts at the end of the week, flowers for Mum and Rose, a poster for me, a matchbox car for Toby. I shudder and grab hold of the corner of my desk to steady myself.

Rose's eyes are like stars. 'Oh, Kirsty-Lee, Kirsty-Lee,' she says, waving the opened letter in front of me. 'Dad wants us to go and stay with him on Monday for the holidays. He couldn't have us before, it was too difficult, but they've got a place of their own now, only a unit but there's a room for us, they've got it all ready. They've a balcony instead of a garden and little potted trees and…'

Very carefully I straighten my pile of books. 'I don't care what they've got,' I say. 'It's nothing to do with me. I'm not going. I'm staying here at Rockvale.'

'Don't be silly. You can't do that. You have to come with me. Dad says…'

'Rose,' I say very quietly. 'Rose, I don't care what you do. Go if you like. But I'm not. Not now. Not ever.' Then my voice breaks and I turn and look at my sister. I want her to understand. Just once I want someone to understand. 'Oh, Rose,' I whisper. 'How can you? How can you even think of going when he…? Don't you care about Mum and…and Toby. He hasn't even invited Toby.'

'What are you going on about, Kirsty-Lee?' says Rose, frowning. 'He asked about Toby, of course he did, but Toby's too young. He's only just turned three. He can't go now, it'd only confuse him. Later, Dad says, when he's older and can understand better. And Mum. What's it got to do with Mum? She's already said we can go. He's our father. Whatever happened between him and Mum and Isla, he's still our father and he loves us.'

I start to shout then. 'Loves us! Listen to yourself, Rose. Just listen to yourself. If he loved us, he'd never have left us. Fathers and mothers, they stay with their children. Both of them. That's what parents are for. That's what it's about. Marriage. Families.'

Rose's cheeks go red. 'Don't shout, Kirsty-Lee! It's not as simple as that and you know it. You always have to make such a ridiculous fuss about everything. That's why everyone has to give into you. Belinda's right. You're spoilt.'

'What's it got to do with Belinda?' I hear my voice rise and I make an effort to keep it steady. 'It isn't her father. She ought to mind her own business and you ought to start thinking for yourself. That's what's wrong with you, Rose Forrester. You don't think for yourself. You just listen to everyone else and then you start crying. You're good at that. Crying. I don't see how you can say I make a fuss when you're the one that's always crying.'

I pause for breath but I haven't finished. Now I've started, I want to go on. Rose's face is white and shocked and her lips are trembling but I don't care. She deserves it. They all deserve it. It's a pity Belinda isn't here as well and Michaela Thornton and... I take a deep breath. I feel suddenly very calm. I'm in control and Rose's face is all blotched and quivering and I'm glad, I'm glad.

'You're stupid, Rose, really stupid.' I say. 'So he writes us a letter. After all these months, he wakes up one morning and remembers us. Big deal. And you're going. Just like that. You're actually going as if nothing's happened, as if...' My voice breaks unexpectedly and I stop.

I'm trembling. I stare at my hands gripping my desk and I don't recognise them. The knuckles are quite white. They look like my mother's hands, my mother's hands when we came home from school in the summer and she held onto the table and told us our father wasn't coming back...

I lift my head to look at Rose again but she's turned away from me so all I can see is the curve of her cheek and her soft, fair hair.

'You don't understand, Kirsty-Lee,' she whispers. 'You don't understand anything at all. You have to...you have to give people a chance. Not everyone's strong like you.'

I don't know what to say. There's too many things inside me. Feelings... I want to be angry, only angry. A moment ago, when I was angry, it felt so good. I want to feel like that again but now...now...

'Please,' says Rose again. 'Please listen, Kirsty-Lee. Think about it. At least think about it. I...I want you to come. If you don't want to come for him, come for me because I...'

I feel something break inside me. 'Are you deaf?' I shout. 'Are you deaf as well as stupid, Rose? I just told you. I'm not going. Not for you. Not for Mum. Not for anyone. I hate him. I hate him and Isla and I'm never going to go and see either of them.' All at once I'm crying. I bite hard at the inside of my cheek till my mouth is full of the taste of blood but I can't make myself stop.

Rose has retreated to the door. 'Kirsty-Lee, I'm sorry. I only meant...'

I keep my back to her and struggle to control myself. 'Go away, Rose,' I whisper at last. 'Go away and leave me alone. I don't want to talk to you.'

As soon as she's gone, I fling myself onto my bed. I'm angry with myself for crying in front of her. I never used to let myself cry. Not for anything. Even when my father left, I didn't. But...but...this feels different. This feels worse. And the things I said. I've never said things like that to Rose before. My sister Rose. I was always so glad she was my sister. Other girls complained about their sisters but I never did. Rose has always been so gentle, so pretty and gentle. She's like her name. When you shut your eyes and say her name out loud, you can see her. Sweet, pretty Rose Forrester. Except now...now...

Rose is just like my father. She has no sense of loyalty. If she goes and stays with him, she'll be no better than he is. She'll be...it'll be like she'll be saying that what he's done isn't so dreadful after all. That's what she meant when she said I had to give him a chance. Only...only...

I put my pillow over my head and sob myself to sleep.

9

Uncle Fred takes Rose to the bus stop. Emma and Belinda and Toby beg to go too so Uncle Fred lets them all scramble in the back. It's not far, just down the road past the general store and the post office. I stand by the gate with everyone else and I force myself to shout goodbye to Rose. Neither of us has mentioned our argument. We've become very careful of what we say to one another, though. I don't like it but I don't know how to make it better. It's worse because of Emma and Belinda. I'm sure, if they weren't always around, Rose and I could have worked things out but I never see Rose by herself any more. It's like she stopped being my sister when we came here. It's like she's their sister instead. Emma's all right, I don't mind her, but I don't like Belinda.

Frowning, I call to Mandy and set off for the old pump house and the swing. The willows on the river bank are bare of leaves. Their branches hang down like the fingers of a giant hand. I sigh. Even the water's changed. It's got secrets now, dark secrets, and along the line of reeds there's a rim of pale scum.

I climb onto the swing and shut my eyes so the magic can take over. As I soar upwards, I hear a voice cry out in triumph. It's not my voice though. It's the little girl Kit. Behind my eyelids the prickles of light turn into pictures. Blue sky. A flowering jacaranda tree. A little boy in a red jumper climbing the ladder of the slippery dip. A woman with a baby in a stroller. My father, his hair falling over his forehead, laughing. I jerk to a stop. My heart is beating too fast. I have to press my hands against it to make it slow down again.

I walk back along the river with Mandy. Close up, the willows look almost sinister. I put a tentative hand out to one but Ash is right. I can't feel the life in it any more. It's gone away till spring. My breath catches in my throat and I lean my cheek against its trunk. I wish I knew how to go with it.

When I get home, I find my mother in the lounge. I don't know where everyone else is. Maybe they're all outside because the house is very quiet. My mother's winding skeins of hand-spun wool into balls and humming to herself. Toby's asleep on the couch, one arm flung across his face. I stand in the doorway watching them. It's like before. Like when my father was still with us. There's a kind of peace about them both.

My mother looks up and notices me. She smiles and I go in.

'That's pretty,' I say, touching the wool. Auntie Evie has dyed it a strange, soft pink.

'It's for Rose,' Mum says. 'We're going to make her a jumper. It'll be a surprise for when she comes back.'

I lean forward as if to examine the wool. That way she can't see my face. 'Do you mind?' I ask. 'Do you mind her going to stay with Dad?'

'Oh, Kirsty-Lee, of course not. How can you think that? He's your father. Nothing can change that. Don't tell me that's why…?'

'He left us.' My voice is fiercer than I intend and I lift my head to look at her. 'Oh, Mum, how can you bear it?'

My mother's lips tremble but she goes on winding the wool. I make myself watch her hands. They're so steady. They give me courage.

'I don't understand,' I whisper. 'I don't understand how Rose can just go on as if…as if what he's done doesn't matter. And…and I don't know why he left. That's what bothers me the most…how he could…'

My mother puts the wool down and lays her hand against my cheek. 'You're grieving, Kirsty-Lee,' she says gently. 'It's all right to grieve. But, but in the end you have to let it go. Otherwise…' She shakes her head. Then she gets up and walks over to the window. Her voice is so soft, I can hardly hear it. 'We were very young when we met, your father and I, he hadn't even finished his apprenticeship, and well, I think what happened was, we just grew into different people, we started wanting different things and that meant…'

I wish I hadn't spoken about it. I've reminded her. I can hear the pain in her voice.

'It's like Toby's kaleidoscope,' she says. 'The pattern keeps changing.'

'No,' I say. 'No. People aren't bits of coloured glass. They…they're alive. They have to put down roots, reach out tendrils to one another. Otherwise, otherwise…'

'I don't know what we are,' my mother says wearily. 'I only know you've got to let things go. Good things. Bad things. When the time comes, you've got to relinquish them. Even you children. You aren't mine or his or anyone's. You belong only to yourselves.' She turns and takes a step or two towards me but I can't bear to look into her eyes any longer so I run to her and put my arms around her instead.

'Things are going to be all right, Kirsty-Lee. For all of us. This is a good place to grow up. I grew up here and so did your Uncle Fred. You like it here, don't you? And sooner or later, I promise you, sooner or later it will stop hurting. You've got your whole life ahead of you, you and Rose and Toby. You mustn't let this one thing spoil it. You'll go out into the world, you'll find people to love, have your own children. Everything.' I feel her arms tighten around me. 'Choices, Kirsty-Lee,' she whispers. 'You'll have choices and sometimes, sometimes the only thing you can do is choose to accept things.' Her voice catches in her throat. 'Otherwise, otherwise you won't be able to bear it.'

I know she's right. But…but I don't know how to do what she says. I don't know how to let things go.

***

Rose sends me a postcard. It's one of those tourist ones with a picture of a New Holland honeyeater and some bottlebrush. I trace around the bird with my finger. I don't want to read it. I don't want to find out what she's been doing with Dad. But in the end, I make myself turn it over.

'Dear Kirsty-Lee,' it says. 'I wish you were here. I miss you. I don't understand why you wouldn't come but that doesn't matter. I was wrong to be angry with you. I love you. Rose. PS Kiss Toby for me.'

I read it several times. I know I have to write her an answer. I don't want to address a letter to Rose at my father's place but I know I have to.

I get up. I hunt through my drawers till I find the stationery set Gran gave me for Christmas. I've never used it. I've never liked writing on fancy paper. Plain old exercise book paper's good enough for me. But Rose likes pretty things and sometimes you have to compromise and do things that other people like.

I don't plan out my letter. I write it quickly because if I think about it too much, I won't know what to say and it will come out all wrong so I put, 'Dear Rose, I liked your card. We have birds like that here on the farm but I expect you know that. It's funny without you. We've never been separated before. I'm sorry I said you were stupid. You're not. I love you too. So does Toby. He keeps asking where you are. I tell him you've gone on a little holiday. We want you to come back soon. Love, Kirsty-Lee'

I read it through. It sounds all right so I put it in its envelope and copy the address from the postcard. Then I get my denim jacket. I'm going to post it straight away before I can change my mind and write something different. It's never easy telling people you love them even when it's just in writing. I've never said it to Rose before unless I said it when I was little and that doesn't count.

I whistle for Mandy. It's a long walk to the post office but Mandy will be upset if I leave her behind. Besides, I need someone to talk to on the way. Talking to Mandy is like writing in here. It's a way of sorting out my thoughts.

Mandy's the best kind of companion. She doesn't demand anything from me. I stop and wait for her to catch up to me. I put my arms around her. 'You're a good girl, aren't you, Mandy?' I say. Her eyes look into mine and she jumps up to lick my face. Then I say aloud, just for practice, 'I love you, Mandy, you silly old dog.' Mandy holds her head to one side and gives a funny sharp bark. You'd almost think she understood.

Emma comes running into my room, her cheeks pink with excitement. 'Jen and Stephanie Mueller just rang up,' she says. 'They want us to go over there tomorrow.'

I look up from the picture I've been trying to draw of Minka but I don't say anything, so Emma goes on.

'They're really nice. You must know them from school, though they don't catch the same bus as us. We always have heaps of fun at their place. They've got an indoor pool, it's heated, so they want us to bring our bathers and everything. They've got a new board game too, they got it last month for Jen's birthday, it's called Pictionary but you can't play it very well with just two, Jen says, that's why it'll be great with the five of us.'

I frown. 'Five of us?'

'Yes, silly. You too of course. They asked you too.'

I put down my pencil. 'I'm not going.'

'Oh, don't say that, Kirsty-Lee! You'll like it there. Really. In the evening, their dad's making a barbecue for us and they're having a bonfire. They've been collecting stuff for ages. We had one when we went there last year. You should have seen it. The sparks were like fireworks. We all pretended they were falling stars and made wishes and...' She stops and looks at me uncertainly. 'Kirsty-Lee, Kirsty-Lee, you will come, won't you?'

I try to keep my voice steady. I don't want to get angry with her. Not like I did with Rose. But people don't listen. They don't listen when you say No. I sigh. 'I just told you, Emma, I'm not going.'

Emma comes closer to me and puts her hand on my arm. 'Please, Kirsty-Lee, please.' Her eyes are all soft and pleading and it's hard to refuse them.

But I have to be strong. I can't go. I don't know what to say to other girls. I'm not interested in the right things. I've listened to them on the bus so I know. Hair and nails and clothes. Boys. I don't think I'll ever be interested in things like that. Especially not boys. Not the way they are. I don't know how to be.

I pick up my pencil and start turning it round and round in my fingers. I don't know what to tell Emma. She doesn't know I'm the wrong kind of girl. Belinda knows by now, and Rose, but Emma's kind of innocent. I don't think she even knows there's two kinds of girls. She likes me so she thinks everyone else will. But she's wrong. I remember Michaela Thornton and the way she looked at me, sort of sneering. It didn't matter to begin with because I had Sam and the other boys I played soccer with but after a while, when Sam and Jason started hanging around her place, it made me feel really bad.

I shake my head and stare helplessly at Emma.

'It's all right, Kirsty-Lee,' she says at last. 'You don't have to come if you don't want to.' She hesitates a moment but, when I don't answer, she goes to my door and opens it.

I jump up. 'Wait, Emma, I…' My heart is beating so fast, I can hardly breathe. I try to make myself say I've changed my mind but the words won't come. I look down at my drawing. 'Thank them,' I whisper. 'They didn't have to ask me. It was nice of them.'

Emma doesn't say anything. She just nods. I've disappointed her. I know I have.

After she goes, I don't feel so good. I'm angry. Not with her. It's me. I used to be so sure of myself. I used to know exactly what I wanted. But now I keep wondering what it would be like if I went. I've seen Jen and Stephanie at school. They're probably all right, no worse than Belinda anyway. And a bonfire. I can imagine it. All dark and the eager flames and a sudden explosion of sparks. They'd be like jewels. Falling stars, Emma said, but they'd be gold instead of silver. I could make a wish, a lot of wishes, one for each of us… For Mum and Rose and Toby. Ash. I could have used my wish for Ash…

I get up and stand by the window. I have to clench my hands hard to stop myself from crying.

***

Emma brings me back a peacock feather from the Muellers. 'They've got heaps of peacocks,' she says. 'You should have seen them strutting across the lawn in the evening.'

I hold the feather up to the light. Its colours gleam blue and green and gold. I shut my eyes and the colours are still there. They've got a life of their own.

Emma looks suddenly anxious. 'You do like it, don't you, Kirsty-Lee? Gran didn't want me to give it to you. She said peacock feathers are bad luck.'

'Bad luck?'

'It's the eye, I think. It watches you but it doesn't protect you. It singles you out for bad things instead.'

I lay the feather carefully across my desk. 'Nothing as beautiful as this could possibly do that,' I say.

Emma smiles. 'That's what I think. I wish you had come. I like Jen and Stephanie but they're more Belinda's friends than mine. It was, it was sort of lonely without you. I kept turning around to tell you things but you weren't there.' She tries to laugh but her eyes are serious. 'We sat around the bonfire and cooked potatoes in the ashes. It was fun.' She runs her finger along the edge of my desk 'Then, then while we were sitting there, laughing, the peacocks started screaming. It sounded so weird. The shadows, the flickering firelight, the stars and behind us, the peacocks. It was like we were suddenly somewhere else. The jungle. I kept looking over my shoulder. The trees. You could see the shapes of the trees but they looked different, sort of menacing. The others didn't notice. I know they didn't. I mean, they heard the peacocks, of course but they didn't know what it meant.' Her hair's fallen over her face and her voice drops to a whisper. 'If you'd been there, Kirsty-Lee, you'd have felt it too.'

45

'Yeah,' I say slowly. I take a deep breath. 'I've never heard a peacock scream.'

Emma pushes back her hair. 'It makes you shiver,' she says. 'Not because you're frightened. It's not that. It's because...' She shakes her head, frowning. 'You know,' she says suddenly. 'I've just thought. They sound like the feather. Exotic. Not like our scrub birds. They're sort of delicate. They blend in. But...'

'Galahs don't. Or cockatoos. They don't blend in.'

'No. No, I guess not. But they still sound right. They belong. Peacocks... Oh, I wish you'd been there, Kirsty-Lee. Then I wouldn't have to explain, you'd know what I mean.'

I bend forward and touch the feather with one careful finger. 'Next time,' I whisper. 'I promise, Emma. I'll come with you next time.'

Emma doesn't say anything but her eyes meet mine and she smiles.

I take Toby to see the horses. There's a paddock not far from us. I found them the day Mandy and I took Rose's letter to the post office. I beg Gran for some carrots and she gives me a whole bunch from the garden. Toby watches me put them in my backpack.

'What else will we take?' I ask him. 'Carrots for the horses, juice for you, a banana each in case we get hungry. What else do we need?'

'Ruggie,' says Toby, holding out the tattered baby blanket he still takes to bed with him.

'All right, Ruggie. Now we'd better get your parka and say goodbye to Mum and find Mandy. Mandy likes the horses. There's a little one too, a foal. Wait till you see it.'

'I want a horse,' says Toby, frowning as I zip up his parka. 'You tell Grandpa, Kirsty-Lee. You tell him to get me a horse and a pig.'

I laugh and take his hand. I feel suddenly happy. The sun comes out. It's rained all morning but now the sun's shining and everything sparkles. Mandy runs ahead of us, her tongue hanging out. She's happy too. It's like she's young again.

We reach the horse paddock at last. It's further than I thought, so Toby's tired and a bit cross. He's all right, though, as soon as I show him the mare with the foal.

'Look, can you see, they're under the trees at the back.'

The mare's dark like the shadows, they almost hide her, but the foal's goldy-brown, it's like sunshine, the light quivers on it. It's the most beautiful thing I've ever seen, all long, spindly legs and a pert, inquisitive face, a wisp of a tail, ridiculous, and little pricked ears. Toby laughs and claps his hands.

The other horses come to the fence. They're ponies, I think, because they're quite small. They've got long tangled manes that make them look like little girls with their hair in their eyes.

'You need hair-ribbons,' I say, pretending to be stern. 'All that messy hair. It needs tying back.' I sound like a teacher. Or Belinda. I grimace at the thought and then I giggle.

The ponies don't care. They toss their heads impatiently as I reach for the carrots. I lift Toby up and he sits on the gate, watching, his eyes big and solemn.

'They're greedy,' he says. 'Aren't they greedy, Kirsty-Lee?'

One of the ponies jerks her head up. Her eyes roll, white-rimmed and wicked, and she nips one of the others so it plunges and kicks out.

Toby clutches hold of the fence post. 'That's naughty,' he shouts, his voice shrill with disapproval. 'Don't you do that. You share.'

At last, when there's no carrots left, they wander back to the mare and foal under the trees.

'Come on then,' I say. 'We've got to go. It's getting late.'

Toby sighs but he climbs down obediently and takes my hand. His hand is so small in mine. Once, he lets go and runs ahead to pick up a piece of quartz from the side of the road. He turns it over, frowning, and gives it to me to put in my backpack. 'That's for Rose,' he says. 'She'll like that won't she, Kirsty-Lee? When she comes back, she'll like that.'

I nod and take his hand again. I like the feel of it in mine.

Mum's at the gate waiting for us. She picks up Toby and balances him on her hip and we go towards the house together. It's almost dark. Behind us the sunset's finishing, a swirl of magenta clouds above the rim of hills and all the paddocks thick with shadows. Once we're inside, though, it's quite different; friendliness and light, everyone laughing and talking, Gran stirring the soup on the stove. I grab up Bambi's bucket and run to find Ash.

Rose comes back from the city. She looks different. Older. She's had her hair cut. Everyone says it looks pretty, the way it curls around her face, but I liked it long. She doesn't look like my sister any more.

She comes into my room to talk to me. She knows I don't want to hear what she's got to say but she comes anyway. 'There's something you've got to know,' she says, sitting down in Emma's chair. 'And you might as well know it now rather than later. It'll give you time to get used to it.'

I don't like this new, determined Rose. I pretend to go on with my drawing so I don't have to answer.

'Look at me, Kirsty-Lee. Stop sulking. This is important. That's why you have to listen. Isla's going to have a baby. That's why Dad left. He had to. He can't let Isla have a baby all by herself. He has to be there for her.'

I put down my pencil and stare at her. 'A baby? How can they be having a baby? They're not even married.'

Rose's cheeks go red. 'Oh, Kirsty-Lee…'

I say, carefully, 'If she's having a baby, it's her fault. She should have thought about it before. He's our father. He…' I lift my chin. 'He already had commitments.'

'It's still his baby. He…'

'Toby's a baby. Or almost. He's still little. And Mum…' My voice wavers for a moment but I force the words out. 'What about you and me, Rose? What about us?'

Rose shakes her head. 'I know. But Isla… He wants to be with Isla. He said she needs him, especially now when…'

'We need him, Rose. Mum…'

'Oh, Kirsty-Lee, it isn't as simple as that. You know it isn't. Things don't

49

always work out the way they should. You've got to try and understand. People, well, they change, things happen, they fall in love. Dad... I don't think he meant to but he did. He fell in love with Isla. And now...' Rose looks down at her hands. 'Isla's nice, Kirsty-Lee. She really is. It isn't her fault. It isn't anyone's.'

I don't say anything. I can't.

Rose lifts her head. She's crying. 'I wish he still loved Mum, Kirsty-Lee,' she whispers. 'I wish it just as much as you do. But he doesn't. It's happened. There's nothing we can do about it.'

For a moment it's very quiet. I watch the shadows on the wall. Outside, a bird calls and is suddenly silent.

'They're going to have a baby,' Rose says, her voice steady again. 'They showed me the photographs from the ultrasound. It's a girl. They already know it's a girl. She'll be our sister.'

I get up and go to my shelf. My spider plant is dying. I don't know why. Maybe it's not getting enough light. I'll have to ask Ash. He'll know. I pull off a dead leaf and crumble it between my fingers.

'She won't be my sister,' I say. 'You're my sister. Just you.'

'Oh, Kirsty-Lee, don't.' She breaks off then. Her eyes, watching me, are full of pity.

I stare at her a moment and then I run to the door and wrench it open. I go down by the river. I don't call Mandy but she follows me all the same. The water's dark and turbulent and I stand by the willows watching it for a long time.

After a while I sit down and clasp my hands around my knees. When I grow up, I'm not going to be like my father. I'm not going to change my mind. The person I choose to love, I'm going to love forever. Whatever happens, whoever else I meet, I'm only going to fall in love once.

I don't let myself think about the baby at all. When my mind skitters towards her, I pick up a stick and throw it into the water. I watch an eddy catch it and whirl it around until at last it sinks out of sight. Then I whistle to Mandy and we go and check on the calves.

I sit by the fire with my knitting. It's raining outside. I've got a cold, not a bad one, but I cough a lot so they won't let me go outside. Ash is mending the fence in the back paddock and I'd rather do that than knit. It's easier. But knitting is useful too, so I make myself concentrate and count the stitches again. You've got to be careful or you end up with too many. Or not enough. Gran's been showing me how to get it right. I'm making Ash a scarf. Auntie Evie's given me all her odd bits of wool for it. I don't use them just at random, though. I'm trying to blend in the colours. Auntie Evie makes dyes from lichen and onion skins and gum leaves and even marigold flowers. They make the wool turn green and yellow and gold and rust-brown. It's like magic.

Emma and Rose and Belinda are doing a jigsaw over at the table. Toby's asleep.

Belinda looks up suddenly, 'Isn't it your birthday soon, Kirsty-Lee? We ought to have a party for you. Mum, don't you think Kirsty-Lee ought to have a party for her birthday?'

Auntie Evie and Mum come in from the kitchen.

Auntie Evie wipes her hands on her apron. 'Yes. Why not? It's a while since we did anything special for any of you girls.'

Everyone starts talking at once.

'We could invite lots of girls from school.'

'Yeah, all the kids in Kirsty-Lee's class but others too, Jen and Stephanie. Boys too. We ought to invite some boys. Hey, Rose, how about we invite Ben…'

'And Petey.'

'A cake. Make one of your chocolate layer cakes, Gran, with mocha icing and fourteen candles. And eclairs and sausage rolls and…'

'Trifle, Mum, a big trifle like we used to have at home. Belinda, you've never tasted anything like Mum's trifle…'

'If the weather's good, we could have a barbecue and we could hang the Christmas lights along the veranda and put the stereo on really loud so we could all hear and…'

'A dress,' says Auntie Evie suddenly. 'Kirsty-Lee will need a dress. I'll make it for you, love. I've got a piece of cream broderie anglaise I've been saving. It'll be perfect with your colouring. A little high-waisted dress gathered in with a draw-string and a flounce around the bottom. You'll have your hair loose. Oh, I can just see it. You'll look beautiful, Kirsty-Lee, all that dark red hair curling round your exquisite little face. No one will recognise you.'

'Mum,' interrupts Belinda. 'Mum, she'll look ridiculous. No one wears dresses like that.'

'You don't, I know, Belinda. I don't think you own a dress any more. But Kirsty-Lee's different. There's no reason why Kirsty-Lee can't…'

I get to my feet. 'I'm not having a party,' I say loudly. 'I don't like parties. They…'

'But you'll be fourteen,' says Auntie Evie. 'That's important, isn't it, girls? It's a turning point. We have to celebrate.'

I'm suddenly desperate. 'No. No. Mum, tell them. I hate parties. Especially ones with lots of people. Tell them, Mum, please.' I pause for breath. 'I'll…I'll run away. I'll run away and hide. Ash'll help me. I'll find a place in the scrub and I'll hide till everyone's gone home. Mum, Mum, you won't let them, will you?'

Mum puts an arm around me and shakes her head ruefully, 'I don't think we'll be having a party, Evie, at least not for Kirsty-Lee.'

'I don't believe it,' says Belinda, disgusted. 'The perfect opportunity for her to make a few friends and she won't even try. She's hopeless.'

The blood stings in my cheeks but I stand my ground. 'I'm not. I just don't like parties. I never have. And it's my birthday, so I ought to be able to choose.' I tilt my chin and glare at Belinda.

Auntie Evie looks upset. 'Well, I don't know, but if you're sure, Kirsty-

Lee. Of course we won't have a party if you really don't want one. But you'd still like a cake, wouldn't you, a cake with candles and a special tea?'

'All right, but that's all. No lights or music or anything. Just a cake.' Then I remember something else. 'And the dress, Auntie Evie. The dress sounds lovely but…well, I'd never get to wear a dress like that, would I? I mean, imagine me feeding the calves in it. It'd be a waste.'

Aunt Evie laughs. 'How about a shirt then, a nice thick shirt? You could wear it under your jacket. You'd be nice and warm then, no matter what the weather was like.'

I nod. She's kind. But she hasn't finished yet.

She looks round at everyone. 'I'm keeping that piece of broderie anglaise for Kirsty-Lee,' she says. 'I know how she'll look in it. Absolutely beautiful. Some day she'll be ready for it. She'll ask me for it and then you'll all see.' She turns and marches back into the kitchen to finish making the scones for afternoon tea.

The girls go back to their jigsaw. But I don't go on knitting. I go to my room instead and unplait my hair. I stand in front of my mirror and brush it out. I want to see if I really do have an exquisite little face. But I look exactly the same as always. Freckles across my nose. Wide dark eyes. Even when I smile, I can't see what Auntie Evie sees. My hair is very thick. It probably would curl if I let it. The little tendrils on my forehead do. That's why I clip them back. Frowning, I pick up my brush and start to redo my plaits.

***

On Monday, I'm well enough to go back to school. We stand at the corner waiting for the bus.

Belinda pulls up the collar of her jacket and fluffs out her hair. 'I really wish you'd let us have a party, Kirsty-Lee,' she says. 'It would have been fun.'

My mouth goes stubborn. 'You can have a party. I'm not stopping you. You just can't have one for me.'

'But you're the one who needs it. It's the only way you're ever going to make friends. I know you're shy but we'd all be there and…'

I interrupt then. 'Shy? I'm not shy.'

'Aren't you? That's what it looks like. You've been going to school with us for months now and you're still wandering around by yourself at lunchtime. I've seen you.'

'I like being by myself.'

'Yeah. Sure.' Belinda's expression changes. Her eyes narrow.

I don't flinch away, though. I face her steadily but my hands, at my sides, clench themselves before I can stop them.

'If you're not shy, then you're up yourself. That's what the other kids say anyway.'

I feel my cheeks get hot. 'I'm not. I…'

'April Wilson says she and Carol Rathjen asked you to have lunch with them but you wouldn't even answer. That sounds like you're up yourself to me. And you wouldn't come with Emma and me to the Muellers even though Jen and Stephanie asked you specially.'

'Belinda, stop it,' says Emma suddenly. 'Mum said you weren't to say anything to her about that.'

Belinda's eyes flick toward her sister's face before they go back to mine. 'She's got to know. It's time someone set her straight. It makes us look bad. You know it does. You. Me. Even Rose.'

At the sound of her name, Rose's head jerks up. She looks from one to the other. 'Me? I wasn't even here. And, and that was ages ago. I really think, Belinda, that you…'

But now she's started, Belinda has no intention of stopping. 'That's not the point. All she ever does is mooch around by herself or go off with Ash. I don't know why your mother allows it. She's fourteen. Fourteen, Rose, and…'

'Shut up,' I shout, surprising even myself. 'Shut up all of you. I'm here. I'm right here. You don't have to talk about me as if I'm not.'

Belinda's voice hisses with venom. 'Oh, yes,' she says. 'Oh, yes, you're here all right and don't we know it. Poor little Kirsty-Lee who's having such a hard time. Well, if you ask me…'

'The bus,' shrieks Emma, grabbing up her bag and running forward. 'Quick, girls, the bus.'

She's made it up. The bus is so far away we can hardly see it. Belinda's mouth tightens but she doesn't say anything. None of us do. We stand in silence, waiting, till the bus pulls up in front of us.

I get on first. I get on first because otherwise I might be tempted not to get on at all.

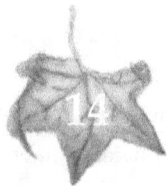

It's my birthday. I wake up very early before it's quite light. I pull on my jeans and an old jumper and go outside. I sit on the veranda steps with Minka on my lap and watch the sky brighten. Fourteen. I don't like the sound of it. It sounds grown up. Fifteen. Sixteen. Seventeen. I don't like the sound of any of them.

I put Minka down and go to find Ash. As soon as we finish our jobs, I go into breakfast by myself. I have the feeling that the best part of the day's over but when I get into the kitchen, I find Mum's made pancakes for a surprise. There's a pile of presents at my place too.

I stand there awkwardly twisting my hands together. Then I take a deep breath. 'I…I didn't expect anything like this,' I say. 'I mean…'

Gran puts her arm around me. 'Why not? It's a special day for all of us, isn't it? Our little girl growing up.'

Toby jiggles up and down on his chair. 'Look at all your presents, Kirsty-Lee,' he says. 'Hurry up and open them. I want to see what you've got.'

'All right. But you'll have to help me.'

I hand him the biggest one and he tears off the paper, shrieking with delight. I get jeans and the shirt Auntie Evie promised and real leather boots like Ash's. Even Belinda gives me something, a little china cat. I hold it in my hand for a moment, suddenly embarrassed. We've haven't spoken since the quarrel. I look up and she catches my eye and pulls a little face and I make myself smile back.

Toby says, 'You haven't unwrapped mine yet, Kirsty-Lee.' He's drawn me another picture, a horse this time.

'I'll hang it next to my cow.' I tell him, laughing. 'Looks like I'm going to end up with my own farm, eh, Toby?'

Auntie Evie glances at the clock. 'Come on, girls, you'd better get a move on or you'll be late. Kirsty-Lee isn't even dressed properly yet.'

'It's your fault, Mum,' says Emma, catching a piece of wrapping paper as it drifts to the floor. 'You should have made her wait till after tea to open her presents. You always do with us.'

'I couldn't,' says Auntie Evie, laughing. 'I couldn't bear to wait that long to see her face. No one's eyes shine like Kirsty-Lee's when she's happy.'

I think about that all day. Auntie Evie seems to know more about me than I do and it's rather disconcerting.

But I'm not sure she's right though. Shining eyes, I'd like to have shining eyes. It sounds like stars. Beautiful. But my eyes are getting like Ash's. I know they are. I've seen them in the mirror and they look inward.

When you're little, it's different. Like Toby. He hasn't any secrets. It's like he runs to people holding out his arms, everyone, whether he knows them or not. I can remember being like that too. Trusting. It's like you're born believing the world's a good place. Except now I know it's not quite like that. People, you can't trust people, not really because although they say all sorts of things, sometimes they stop meaning them and so you can never be sure.

Auntie Evie said it herself when she was talking about the party. Fourteen's a turning point. You can't ever go back. Toby's got shining eyes. I saw them this morning when he was helping me was open my presents. But mine. Auntie Evie's wrong. I'm too old to have shining eyes.

It's evening. It's been raining all day but it's stopped now and the garden is suddenly at peace. I can hear Ash playing his guitar. It sounds different tonight, though. Moonlight on water, I think, and I go slowly down the veranda steps so I can hear it better. Ash's music is like that; it calls to you.

As soon as he sees me, Ash stops playing. 'Kirsty-Lee,' he says. 'I've been hoping you'd come. They told me it was your birthday the other day and I've got something for you.'

I nod and Ash puts down his guitar. It's almost dark but over in the west the humps of the hills are still outlined with gold. Ash opens the door of his room and in the sudden spill of light, he's silhouetted, a dark shape like the hills in front of us. I sit down next to his guitar and prop my chin on my hands. When he comes back, he doesn't close his door again but leaves it open so we can see. He's got something in his hands, a little wooden box and, smiling, he puts it carefully in my lap. I run my finger over its lid. It's got blue flowers painted on it and a border of intricate, carved leaves.

'It's pretty,' I say. 'Really pretty.'

Ash looks away from me. 'Tamara liked it,' he says. 'She kept jewellery in it. She'd like you to have it. That's why I decided to give it to you.'

'Tamara?'

'My sister. My little sister. She was like you, Kirsty-Lee.' His mouth goes taut. 'Or maybe that's just what I tell myself. Maybe she wasn't like you at all.' He reaches over to touch the box. His hand trembles. 'Sometimes I pretend you're her, Kirsty-Lee. I don't think she'd mind. She'd be glad. I'm sure she'd be glad.'

I don't know what to say, so I stare out into the gathering darkness and wait.

'I killed her,' says Ash suddenly. 'I killed them all, my best friend Bart, little Sheila Davidson, she was only sixteen, and my sister Tamara. For years and years I've wished I killed myself as well.'

I catch my breath. My chest hurts. My chest hurts so much I can hardly breathe. 'Ash,' I whisper. 'Ash.'

'I can't escape from it. Not ever. It goes on and on and I keep seeing it. Every detail. The blue dress Sheila wore, the way she tipped her head back when she laughed. I'd given her some little gold earrings, they were shaped like flowers and she'd worn them for the first time that night. Tamara and Bart were very quiet. I knew why. Tamara had told me Bart wanted to marry her but she'd told him she wouldn't. "I'm too young," she said. "I love him but I'm too young. Oh, Ash, I want to live a bit first." She didn't know, how could she, she'd no more time left. She'd used it all up. They all had and I...' Ash turns to me. His pupil are so dilated, his eyes look black.

'Please,' I whisper. 'Please.' But he doesn't hear me. I know he doesn't.

'It was dark. No moon, not even any stars There was a mist though, it kept coming and going...treacherous...and the road, I thought I knew it but that night it seemed to go on forever, winding in and out of the hills and so narrow... I don't know, I must have misjudged a turn. Sheila was laughing and I couldn't help it, I turned to look at her, her sweet little face. We hit a tree and then we skidded and went right off the road, somersaulted into the gully below. I heard them scream... Oh, the screaming...After a while, Sheila was quiet but Bart and Tamara...all through the night I heard them. I couldn't do anything. I was trapped. I couldn't even move. In the morning the light came, so soft and gentle and all the birds began to sing. But by then I knew it was over. They'd stopped, some time in the night they'd stopped screaming. It was hours before I was found. Hours. And all that time I tried to decide which was worse, the sound of them screaming or the dreadful, dreadful silence when they stopped.' He puts his head down on his knees and starts to sob.

I can't bear it. I put my arms around him and hold him. It's like he's Toby, Toby crying in the night after one of his dreams and I have to hold him till he stops.

'It's over,' I whisper. 'It was a long time ago. Ash, please. It's over.' I don't know what to do. I want to go back to my room where Minka's waiting, where it's safe, my books, the pictures Toby's drawn me, my spider plant, everything familiar. But Ash. I can't leave Ash. I don't know what to do but I can't leave Ash.

After a while, he's himself again. He doesn't say anything. He just straightens up, reaches for his guitar and begins to play. His music aches and throbs, it rises to a crescendo, then just when I think I can't bear any more, it changes and a gentleness comes into it. I think of petals drifting, white petals in the wind. It gets inside me and at last I'm quiet again.

Ash turns to me. 'I'm sorry, Kirsty-Lee. I shouldn't have told you. You're only a kid and...'

'No.' I lift my chin. 'No, it's all right. We're friends, Ash, and friends tell one another things, even hard things. Otherwise...otherwise, well, they're not really friends at all.'

Ash nods slowly. His eyes are very clear now. They're like Toby's eyes. Trust, I think; Ash trusts me.

I want to say more. I want to tell Ash how important he is to me but I don't know the right words so I trace around the flowers on my box instead. 'I'm glad you gave me this, Ash,' I whisper. 'Thank you.'

Ash picks up his guitar again and I close my eyes and lean against him.

There's a new calf. Ash comes up to the house to tell me and I run down with him to look at it. It's still with its mother. She lifts her head for a moment but, when she sees it's only us, she goes back to licking it. It struggles to its feet and looks around, astonished. It switches its tail and takes a few staggering steps. Then, as if suddenly remembering something important, it thrusts its little black muzzle under her, finds her udder and begins to suck. My throat tightens in pity. Tomorrow Ash will take it away and put it with the others. That's what happens with dairy cows. 'They don't mind,' says Uncle Fred. 'They're bred not to mind.' But Ash and I know better.

I turn to go back inside. I can't do anything about the calf. I know that. But I can still feel sorry. I lift my chin. At least, I can feel sorry.

Rose meets me at the gate. 'Kirsty-Lee, Kirsty-Lee, Dad's just rung up. The baby's come. She was born this morning.' She pauses and looks at me expectantly but, when I don't respond, she goes on, her voice trembling with excitement. 'They've called her Charlotte. Charlotte Rose.' She drops her head then and bites at her lip. 'I didn't ask them to. It was Isla's idea. She thought I'd like it.'

I push past her. I can't be bothered listening to any more. I go into my room and slam the door.

***

When I get home from school, there's a letter from my father. Mum doesn't say anything about it; she just leaves it propped it up on my desk against my clock. I know it's from him even though he's typed the address.

He can't fool me. I recognise the postmark. Acacia Park. That's where he lives now, that's where his unit is, the one Rose kept talking about, the one with the balcony and the windows with wooden shutters. That's where he lives with Isla and the baby.

I don't open the letter, though. I don't even touch it. But, when I'm getting ready for bed that night, I suddenly snatch it up and hold it, panting, against my chest. Then, very slowly and carefully, I tear it in half. There's a photo inside, a photo of a baby. Before I can stop myself, I see a corner, some sort of dark background and a little starfish hand. My heart starts to beat very fast and I tear it across again and again. At last, triumphant, I drop the pieces in my rubbish bin. I will not have my father or the baby or Isla in my life. I have made up my mind to it.

But during the night, I wake up. I lie there in the dark and start to remember things. I remember when Toby was born and Dad took us to the hospital to see him for the first time. They had him in an incubator to begin with because he'd had trouble breathing. He had a lot of dark hair and he was so small and spindly, all little thrusting arms and legs and they let us put our hands in to touch him because they said he needed to know he belonged to us.

I ache suddenly for my baby sister. It isn't her fault. My father and Isla chose but the rest of us didn't. I ache because I'll never hold her. I'll never sit with her in my lap, rocking her, while I wait for Mum to come home. I'll never take her to see the horses in the paddock down the road or hang up the pictures she's drawn above my desk. I'll never see her. I can't. I've decided. I can't do it any other way. One little starfish hand…

I fling my arm across my face. I don't want to think about it any more. But I can't help myself. I let myself whisper her name in the darkness. Charlotte. Charlotte Rose Forrester. I don't know why her name sounds so sad.

We're doing the dishes. It's one of Gran's rules. 'We get the meal. You girls clear up afterwards.' I don't mind, though I'd rather do outside things. Still, fair's fair. Belinda's washing up; it's her turn. Rose and Emma dry. I clear the table.

Rose starts talking about the baby. I know why she's doing it. She wants me to hear. I prim up my mouth. It isn't right. It isn't honest and I intend to tell her so. But not now. Not in front of Emma and Belinda. It isn't anything to do with them. It's private.

Rose says, 'And guess what? Dad says Charlotte's got red hair, just like Kirsty-Lee.'

I stop wiping down the benches and stand very still. I have to concentrate on holding myself rigid because if I move, I…

Emma laughs. 'Oh, how cute,' she says. She doesn't mean anything by it. I know she doesn't. She turns to Belinda, her face wistful. 'Oh, Belinda, I wish we had a baby sister like Rose and Kirsty-Lee.'

I can't believe what she is saying. Emma. Emma, who's my friend. I go up to her. I go right up to her and I say slowly and carefully, 'You don't know what you're talking about, Emma. Do you want to know how we got our baby sister, Rose and me? Do you want to know what our father did? He found someone, some woman who wasn't our mother and they…'

I shake my head. There's no way I can say it. But I don't have to. The words are already in the room with us. Emma and Rose and Belinda, they can hear them too because I see them drop their eyes. The colour mounts painfully in Emma's cheeks.

'So, Emma,' I say. 'So are you sure, really sure, you want a baby sister like ours?'

Emma sucks in her breath. Her eyes are wide and frightened. 'Kirsty-Lee, I...'

Something breaks inside me. I rush at her and slap her. I slap her hard. I lift my hand to do it again. It feels so good. All these months, all these interminable months I have felt so much, too much, and now at last, at last...

Belinda grabs hold of me. 'You bitch,' she hisses. 'You vicious little bitch.'

'Leave me alone,' I shout, kicking out at her. 'Leave me alone.'

'Kirsty-Lee, Kirsty-Lee,' whimpers Rose. 'Stop it, oh, stop it.'

Suddenly the room's full of people. Their faces press in on me and I put up my hands to ward them off. Mum. Mum. I want my mother. I open my mouth to scream but it's all right. I'm in her arms. I'm safe. I hide my face against her dress and I start to cry and it's like I'm never going to be able to stop. Everyone's talking at once. Gran. Auntie Evie. Belinda. Rose. But Mum's on my side. She understands. She makes them all go away. Belinda's shouting. 'But it isn't fair. She shouldn't be allowed to get away with it,' and Mum holds me in her arms and rocks me and her arms are fierce and protective and she won't let them hurt me. None of them can hurt me because my mother's got hold of me and she won't let them.

'It's the baby, isn't it?' she whispers at last, her lips against my hair. 'You're upset about the baby, aren't you, Kirsty-Lee?'

I nod and take a deep, shuddering breath.

'Cry all you want,' she says and her voice starts to rise. 'Cry if it helps and while you're about it, cry for me too, for, oh God, oh God, I don't know how I can bear it either.' She stops. She's shocked at what she's said. She puts her hand over her mouth. Her eyes meet mine and I tighten my arms around her neck.

'It's all right, Mum,' I whisper and I lay my cheek against hers. 'It doesn't matter. You don't have to be brave in front of me. I...oh, Mum, it's only Kirsty-Lee, don't you remember, only me. You can say what you like in front me.'

My mother sighs. 'Oh, Kirsty-Lee, I don't think any one knows how I feel, how I really feel. They think…it's been months…they think I should be over it by now…a new life but…' Her lips quiver. 'I've tried so hard since we came here, been brave for you children, laughed and made plans with Gran and Evie, pretended and all the time, all the time I've hoped… But he'll never come back now, Kirsty-Lee, how can he? He might have got over Isla, she's so much younger than him, a passing fancy, but a baby…the baby will be between us forever. Even if he could, I'd never be able to forget the baby.'

'Rose,' I whisper. 'Rose said… She's glad about the baby, Mum. She says, she says she's our sister and…'

'Oh, Kirsty-Lee, it isn't the baby's fault. You mustn't blame her. A little baby. Oh, promise me, Kirsty-Lee, you won't blame the baby. That wouldn't be fair.'

I wipe my face with the back of my hand. 'I know,' I say. 'I know it isn't her fault. It's just…'

My mother has turned her face away. She doesn't speak for a while and when she does, her voice is so low I can hardly hear it. 'I can't, I can't even blame your father. I wish I could. It would be easier. Oh, if only I could hate them. Your father. Isla. The baby. Even the baby. It would be so much easier if I could hate them.' She puts her hand up and presses it against her mouth. 'I can't. I can't make myself hate them, even though…'

All at once I can't bear any more. 'I know,' I say. 'I know.' I get up and go over to the window. The sky's quite dark and I can see all the stars. My mother comes and stands next to me. She reaches for my hand. We stand there for a long time watching the sky and holding one another's hands.

***

I feel bad about Emma. I go into the bathroom and wash my face and then I replait my hair. I stare at myself in the mirror but, apart from my swollen eyes, I look much the same as always. I make a face at myself and go and look for Emma. I don't want to but I know I have to. Not only for her. For myself too.

She's with the others in their room. I stand in the doorway a moment but none of them notice me or, if they do, they pretend not to. I square my shoulders and march in. Emma's sitting on her bed, reading. She's got her head bent down but I can still see the red mark I made on her cheek.

I go right up to her and I say, 'I'm sorry I hit you, Emma. I'm sorry I said what I did. I shouldn't have. It was wrong of me.' The words don't sound right. They sound stiff and formal as if someone has told me to say them but I don't know how to make them sound right.

'It's a pity you didn't think about that before you did it,' Belinda says. 'If I had a temper like yours, I'd try harder to control it.'

I ignore her; she's not important.

Emma flushes. 'Let's forget about it, Kirsty-Lee. It doesn't matter.'

But I know better than that, so I lift my head and make my eyes meet hers. 'It does,' I say steadily. 'It matters because I like you and I hurt you and I wish I hadn't.'

Emma nods. But she smiles too. Her smile's like my mother's. Reassuring. I take a step or two toward her. There's so much I want to say, to explain. About my mother. And my father. Most of all I want to tell her about my father. How he loved us and then he... I want her to understand.

But Belinda's there. And Rose. And, and even if they weren't... I shake my head. There are some things I can never tell anyone.

'I'm sorry,' I say again. Then I turn quickly and run back to my own room.

***

Emma's makes Minka a little grey felt mouse. I sit next to her and watch. She's got clever hands. It's got black beads for eyes and a long pink tail. She even embroiders whiskers on its face. Minka loves it. Auntie Evie gives us a bell to put inside it so that when Minka pounces on it, it will jangle. Minka's astonished. Her stiff little whiskers bristle with indignation. Then she reaches out a cautious paw and bats it again. Emma and I look at one another and laugh.

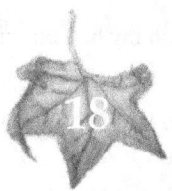

It's dark. Minka wakes me up. She taps my cheek with her paw and chirrups. She wants to go outside. I stumble to the door and open it. The garden is full of moonlight. It drifts like silver mist and I stand, shivering, in my bare feet, enthralled. For a moment, I'm tempted to follow Minka. I take a step forward but then I stop. I don't belong there. It's a different world.

Ash is playing his music. I've never heard it so late before. It drifts like the mist and has the same unearthly beauty. It catches hold of me and makes me want to listen to it forever. But at last it stops and I hear Ash close his door. I sigh. I don't understand how I feel. It's as though I've lost something, something unbelievably precious and my throat aches with the loss of it.

Minka comes running to me out of the shadows and I pick her up. It's like we've both been under a spell and now it's broken.

I go back to bed but I can't fall asleep again.

My father isn't married to Isla. They have to wait till January when the divorce comes through. I don't see how that'll make any difference, though. After all, being married didn't make him stay with my mother.

I get scared thinking about it. I get scared for Charlotte. Because what if Dad doesn't marry Isla? What if he finds someone else to fall in love with? What will happen to her then? A little baby.

I bite down hard on my lip. I don't want to think about her. She isn't my sister. She isn't anything to do with me. I've already decided that.

Only…my father can't be trusted. We know that. My mother and Rose and me. Even Toby. Probably Isla knows it as well. But Charlotte doesn't. And she'll grow up and she'll start to love him and she'll expect him always to be there and then one day she'll come home from school and…

I sit up suddenly and push my hair out of my eyes. It's nothing to do with me. I get out of bed and turn on my light. My jacket's slung over my chair and I struggle into it and put on my boots. As soon as I get outside, I whistle for Mandy. I look up at the sky. It's brilliant with stars. I squint up my eyes and they run together into silver splinters of light.

I pull up the collar of my jacket and walk down to the river. I find my way to the abandoned pump house and the old swing. I get on and I start to work my legs. I don't let myself think. I concentrate on making the swing go higher and higher. The stars are so far away. They've seen so much. Pain and terror. Great joy. Birth and death. Everything. And it hasn't changed them. They go on shining. Being themselves.

After a while I'm so cold, I have to go back. I feel better, though. I fling myself face down on my bed and fall instantly to sleep.

In the morning I go to find Rose. She's brushing her hair in front of the mirror and smiling at her reflection.

I clench my hands in my pockets and ask her if I can have one of her photos of the baby. 'I'm not putting it in a frame or anything like you have,' I say. 'But I would like to have one. Just…just to keep.' I fiddle with the bottles and jars on the dressing table she shares with Emma and Belinda. 'I've been thinking,' I say. 'You've got two families now, haven't you? Dad and Isla and…and Charlotte as well as me and Mum and Toby.'

Rose looks hard at me. 'You have too, Kirsty-Lee. It's not that hard.'

'It is for me. I…' I swallow. 'If I was like you and visited him, I'd feel like…like I was betraying Mum and Toby and…'

'But, Kirsty-Lee, that's silly. Mum wouldn't mind. She'd be glad. She's worried about you, the way you've cut yourself off from everything. And….oh, Kirsty-Lee, don't you see, you have to forgive Dad.'

'I can't. Oh, Rose, I can't.'

But Rose doesn't understand. She shakes her head. 'You have to. You can't hold it against him forever.'

But I can. I know I can. I'm not soft and loving and gentle like Rose.

Or Mum. Mum doesn't blame him but I…I'm not like Mum and Rose. I wish I was.

***

It's Saturday. I take the calf buckets back to the kitchen and go and find Ash. He's down by the river. Spring is coming. The branches of the willows have buds on them. They're a delicate pale green and I reach out and touch one. All of spring is so vulnerable. It aches inside me.

I sit down next to Ash. 'Do you think I should forgive my father?' I ask.

Ash takes a while to answer. He's watching the water. It's still dark and angry. It isn't ready yet to relinquish its power to spring.

At last he says, 'Forgiveness isn't easy, Kirsty-Lee. Sometimes it takes a lifetime.'

I know what he means. He's remembering Tamara and the others. He's thinking it will be a lifetime before he can forgive himself for what happened to them.

I say quietly, 'I'm not sure I want to forgive him. I'm not sure I can.'

Ash looks at me. His eyes are no longer opaque. I can see right inside him. I can see his pain.

'You love him, Kirsty-Lee,' he says. 'You love your father. That's why it's so hard. You can't stop loving him.'

I start to protest but then I stop. I know he's right. All these months, I've been fighting against it. I love my father. It's as simple as that. I'll always love him. I can't help it.

'Oh, Ash,' I whisper. 'Oh, Ash what am I going to do?'

Ash leans toward me and traces the line of my cheek with his finger. His eyes are very sad. 'You'll live, Kirsty-Lee. You'll live like the rest of us. One day at a time. And it'll get easier. That's all I can promise you. It will get easier.'

One of the calves, the little one I called Pixie, dies. Ash tried everything he knew but he couldn't save her.

'White scour,' he says, sighing. 'It's hard to cure.' He strokes her gently.

She was so pretty, like a fawn I'd thought, with delicate legs and big, shy eyes. I kneel beside her while Ash goes to get the spade and the wheelbarrow. Dead she looks shrunken. Something's gone out of her. The life force. We bury her under the liquidambars.

I go into the hay shed to think. It isn't the calf. I'm sorry about her of course. But Ash has given her back to the earth. 'Where she belongs,' he said, breaking off a handful of young leaves and scattering them over her grave. It's the word 'belongs' that haunts me. Always the word 'belongs'. It reminds me of what I've lost. It reminds me of before.

The thing is, I'm not Kit any more. I haven't been her for a long time, not since I came here. But I can remember her. I can remember how good it felt, waking up in the morning, knowing what to expect, knowing, most of all, who I was.

I pull at the bale of hay I'm sitting on. It's coarse and prickly and smells musty. I used to think hay smelt only of summer. But summer was a long time ago. Maybe that's why the hay no longer smells good. It's too old… I sigh. I'm Kirsty-Lee now. She sounds like the kind of girl who wears lacy dresses and ties her hair back with ribbons. She's got an exquisite little face and she smiles a lot and flirts with the boys on the bus. On the weekend, she and her sister walk to the general store. They sit outside eating ice cream and Jen and Stephanie Mueller and Ben Wilson join them and they all spend the afternoon together, laughing in the sunshine. I don't want to do these things, though. Or do I? I'm not sure. That's what bothers me. Not being sure. Kit was always so sure.

I hear Ash come in but I don't move. Anyone else, even Emma, and I'd have jumped up and pretended I had something important to do. But I trust Ash. I don't have to hide anything from him.

Ash sits down next to me. 'You upset about the calf?' he asks. 'No good grieving, not for her.'

'I know.' Then abruptly I add, 'It's not her. It's me.'

Ash nods. Light falls on us through the open doorway and we watch the dust motes dancing in it. When I was little, my father told me they were fairies. For the first time, I remember him without pain.

'I've been thinking about names,' I say. My voice sounds brittle and for a moment it distracts me. But Ash's silence reassures me. He's easy to tell things to. 'Take Rose, for example. If they gave you a name like Rose, you'd have to turn out beautiful, wouldn't you? I mean…'

'Maybe.'

'Kirsty-Lee is such a stupid name,' I burst out. 'It's so…so pretentious.'

Ash shrugs. 'I don't think so. I like it. If you say it often enough, it sounds like a bird call. Anyway, it doesn't matter. It's not the name that makes you who you are.'

I bend my head and examine the hay again. 'That's the trouble,' I whisper. 'I don't know who I am. I used to but…' I break off.

Ash turns my face toward him. His hands are so gentle. Whenever he touches anything that's little and defenceless, you can trust his hands to be gentle. 'It's all right, Kirsty-Lee,' he says. 'It takes time. No one knows who they are right off. You have to grow into yourself, bit by bit.' He smiles and his eyes look into mine. 'You know what I think, Kirsty-Lee? I think you'll find yourself worth waiting for.'

I lean against him. I'm safe with him. It's not like I thought. When you love someone, you give them pieces of yourself. I did that with my father and he went away. But he left me something too. Something of himself. Little things perhaps. Memories. I'm not sure yet.

And Ash. Ash has given me so much. Faith. Isn't that it? Faith in life itself. He's my kind of person. That's the important thing. Maybe finding out about yourself includes finding out about the kind of people you belong with. And I've found Ash. We understand the same things. And I'll be able to find others. I don't have to be always alone. It's simple really.

All at once I start to smile. It's going to be easier than I thought, becoming Kirsty-Lee.

www.ingramcontent.com/pod-product-compliance
Lightning Source LLC
Chambersburg PA
CBHW071543100726
47908CB00004B/1491